Loose Ends
IN
Western Literature

Michael Skupin

For my beloved wife

Florence Chen

Preface

This book is a collection of essays, talks and conference papers on literary and pedagogical questions that are off the beaten track. They have no unifying thread, so I have not attempted to organize them chronologically or topically. Freedom is a noble thing.

In addition to the "old reliables" that I have thanked in previous works, it is with pleasure that I name new benefactors who have helped my efforts over the last year: my Chinese Culture University colleagues, Clio Sun, Lucy Yao, Tim Fox and Kid Lam; my counterparts at other universities on the western edge of the Pacific, Beatrice Lei, C. H. Perng, Francis So, John McKenny and Roshni Mooneeram; in the United States, Neil Bernstein, Robert Cape, Jim Johnson, Donna Campbell and Scott Donaldson; and Stefan Schomann and Wu Hui of Berlin and Beijing. For their advice and encouragement, my sincere thanks.

Michael Skupin
Houston and Taipei
September 29, 2009

Table of Contents

A False Etymology in *Moby-Dick*

I knew no Hebrew the first time I read Moby-Dick, and so paid no attention to the note in Melville's "Etymology." Thirtysomething years later, however, during a graduate seminar, I noticed that my edition gave a Hebrew word for "whale" that in fact meant no such thing. A quick survey of other editions used by my fellow-students revealed that each edition had a different word, and that all were wrong. A visit to the library yielded more variants still.

(The reader may be aware that Hebrew writes consonants, or if you will, Hbrw wrts cnsnnts, which I romanize with capital letters; I supply the vowels lower-case.)

1. תר (Modern Library). תר (T[o]R) could be read as "dove," although that word is usually written תור (ToWR). The alert reader may identify this with the onomatopoeic Latin turtur, the English turtledove.

2. חן (W.W. Norton and Russell & Russell). חן (KheN) means "favor."

3. תך (Oxford University Press). תך (ToKh) means "deceit."

4. תן (Library of America). תן (TaN) refers to an unknown wilderness animal. In the Authorized ("King James") Version the word is translated "dragons," but since it is spoken of as howling and sniffing, it would rather appear to have been a canine. It is important for our purposes here to note that only the plural is found in the Bible, so this singular is an inferential form.

5. תו (Dodd, Mead and Company). תו (TaW) is the garden-variety word for the Hebrew letter "T."

6. תז (Everyman). The letters are romanized TZ, and mean nothing that I know of.

I imply no criticism of the editors of these editions. It is evident that whatever Melville wrote was illegible, so each editor was right to take his best guess and leave it at that.

The editors of two other editions, however, try to go beyond the vanishing point, with results that require commentary. The first, Charles Feidelson, Jr. (also of the חן school), implies that there is more than meets the eye when he writes in a footnote[1] that "Melville's Hebrew appears to be in error." In other words, he is saying that "favor" *appears* not to mean "whale." There is no appears about it: Melville made a mistake, pure and simple, just as when in *The Encantadas* the Spanish redondo ("round") is written "rodondo." When he wrote French or Latin words he was quite exact, which is to be expected: Sealts' *Melville's Reading* tells us that Melville's library included various books in French and Latin, the "spell-checkers" of the day; there were no reference works in Spanish. Either he was satisfied with an approximation of the Spanish word or he relied on memory, with a garnish of hubris. As far as can be known, Melville's library contained not one word of Hebrew.

He made a mistake.

Editors Luther S. Mansfield and Howard P. Vincent evidently have a problem with this,[2] and look for profundity. They begin by saying that "Melville was no Hebrew scholar," but then contradict themselves by proceeding as if he had been just that, or at least that "with the aid perhaps of some scholarly friend he was diligently attempting to get the most inclusive Hebrew term, one that would evoke for him all of the significant Biblical allusions to the whale." All! A tall order, even for a Hebrew super-scholar!

Fortunately, there is a piece of evidence that settles the matter, and shows where Melville was led astray. The generic Hebrew word for sea-monster is תנין (TaNiYN) or תנים (TaNiYM). It takes no knowledge of Hebrew at all to notice that these words have four letters,

---

[1] Feidelson 5
[2] Mansfield 579

but that Melville's shape-shifting word in "Etymology" has only two. Here is the clue, and one doesn't have to be any kind of Hebrew scholar at all to follow it. Both words are grammatically singular, and (as a little library work reveals) were correctly identified as such in the Hebrew reference works available in Melville's day – with one exception, which is our smoking gun. First published in 1843 and frequently reprinted (1857 saw the fifth edition), *The Englishman's Hebrew and Chaldee Concordance of the Old Testament* has two תנים's, one for the whale and the other for the wilderness critter mentioned above, the תן (TaN), which, the reader will recall, is found only in the plural in the Bible. The reader will recall the plural ending from the well-known cherub-cherubim, seraph-seraphim. Melville evidently looked up "whale" in the "English and Hebrew Index" on p. 1459 and found תנים, then dutifully turned back to p. 1352 for examples of its use. The landlubber תנים comes up first, and must therefore have been the first word that Melville's eye lit on. There, among the "dragons" – and here's the giveaway – there is an out-of-place "whale" תנים. Evidently taking this misidentification at face value, along with the note that the word only occurs in the plural, our author evidently asked himself: if the word is plural, then what is the singular? A rough-and-ready knowledge of the Hebrew masculine plural (cherub-cherubim, seraph-seraphim) and a dash of hubris led him to attempt a back-formation from תנים, that is, תן (TaN) + ם׳ - (-iM), yielding an incorrect תן (TaN). It was a false etymology, however, leading to the editorial Babel cited above. The author's handwritten two-letter תן has been misread many editors in many ways, simply because there is no right way to read it.

Gambling in *The House of Mirth*

James Bond has an unusual mission in Ian Fleming's *Moonraker*: he must play bridge. A cheat has insinuated himself into the club of Bond's superior, and 007's task is to expose him. Their face-off over the card table is an exciting one, both from the standpoint of bridge tactics and of characterization: Fleming has the villain gradually drop his mask of gentility as his fortunes fade, and the transformation is artful and convincing.

Lily Bart must also play bridge. The plot of Edith Wharton's *The House of Mirth* turns on her luck at the gaming table: the cards turn against her, and the financial pressure from her gambling debts makes her membership in her ritzy social set all too tenuous, and begins the process of her ruin. Yet the bridge games that are so central to the plot happen offstage, as it were: Wharton makes no effort to describe them, even though she must have sensed the dramatic and characterizational opportunities they offered; she may even have known firsthand a fine treatment of the subject, that of Alphonse Daudet in his short story "Un Membre du Jockey Club," to be discussed later. If Ian Fleming could use this game of chance for a convincing delineation of psychology and motivation, what might Wharton have achieved with a face-off between Lily and Bertha Dorset? A polished as *The House of Mirth is,* this omission could not have been accidental. I argue that Wharton had a fine sense of topicality, and that she intended to avail herself of several hot topics of her day, which, as we shall see, her readers lumped under the heading of gambling, and that she was astute enough not to overdo it. Considering the passions that her topics evoked, less was more.

When Edith Wharton made gambling the cause of Lily's money woes, she tapped into a deep reservoir of passion on the subject of wagering. As early as 1812, one M.L. Weems had published a tract titled *God's revenge against gambling exemplified in the miserable lives and untimely deaths of a number of persons from both sexes, who had sacrificed their health, wealth, and honor at the gaming tables.* A sampler, for the sake of tone:

> Poor distracted Girl!   She is thinking, though now, alas! too late, of the bright honors once placed within her reach... But alas!   deceived [sic]   by demons whom she mistook for friends, she was led to a *gaming table,* which, in a few feverish years, swallowed up all!   Not leaving even a wreck [sic] behind!   Her bloom, her beauty, her fame, fortune all, all, sacrificed to the most *detestable of vices!...*[1]

Even without considering external evidence, one recalls that in *HoM* the "whisper campaign" against Lily is focused on her alleged bridge mania, and the anger this elicited is exemplified by Mrs. Peniston. After expressing indifference to Lily's other expenditures, she comes to a boil when she hears

> "...but then there are her gambling debts besides..."
> "Gambling debts?   Lily?"   Mrs. Peniston's voice shook with anger and bewilderment.   She wondered whether Grace Stepney had gone out of her mind.   "What do you mean by her gambling debts?"
> "Simply that if one plays bridge for money in Lily's set one is liable to lose a great deal — and I don't suppose that Lily always wins."
> "Who told you that my niece played cards for money?"

---

[1]   "Vignettes" 1

"Mercy, cousin Julia, don't look at me as if I were trying to turn you against Lily! Everybody knows she is crazy about bridge...but I'm sure I'm sorry I spoke, though I only meant it as a kindness."

To get an idea of the images that the mention of games of chance evoked in the minds of the readers of Wharton's day we consider two sources, one pro-gambling, the other anti-. The first window on the times is found in an enormously interesting collection of observations and anecdotes about many forms of gambling and in several countries: *Light Come, Light Go: Gambling—Gamesters—Wagers—The Turf,* by one Ralph Nevill, was published only five years after *HoM*, and provides vivid contemporary perspective. It is a gambler's-eye view of games of chance from America to Monte Carlo, and is full of details about various forms of wagering and anecdotes about society's reactions to them. Bridge, the cause of Lily's downfall, is mentioned specifically.

High bridge is now played in London mostly by wealthy people, well able to take care of themselves. The outcry raised some time ago about young girls being compelled to join in playing for large stakes is not based on a solid foundation of truth, for as a rule high players are not fond of running the chance of drawing a novice as a partner. A bad player spoils the game.[2]

Lily is no bad player, of course; her circle welcomes her as a fourth; her skill notwithstanding, her luck runs out. Nevill gives more background on the London scene; we may generalize, since it could not have been much different from the New York scene.

---

[2] Nevill 135

Though there is practically no gambling in West-End clubs, a good deal of baccarat and poker is occasionally played in private houses, ladies being not infrequently amongst the players, and here gaming assumes its most undesirable form. Temper as well as money is generally lost, whilst the winners are exposed to a by no means remote probability of never being paid.   Private gambling is especially dangerous to young men, and without doubt a thousand times more harm is done by play of this sort than by all the properly conducted public tables in the world.[3]

Some skepticism is called for on Nevill's last point, given the evidence of an earlier literary vignette involving just such a public table, Daudet's short story "Un Membre du Jockey Club" (possibly known to Francophile Wharton), in which a visiting city slicker fleeces a small-town dandy at cards.   In Daudet's story the loser's frenzy of despair is forcefully depicted; he is saved from ruin by the Parisian's *beau geste* of abruptly returning the money lost:

> *Il vida ses poches sur la table, et, quittant lui aussi pour une minute son masque de gandin, il dit d'une voix naturelle et bonne: «Reprends donc ça, imbécile...Est-ce que tu crois que nous jouions sérieusement?»*
> ("He emptied his pockets on the table, and, also abandoning for a moment his mask of the dandy, he said in a voice natural and good, "Take it back, then, fool... Do you think that we were playing seriously?")

Daudet's ram-in-the-thicket ending is especially strong because his readers knew full well that this was not the way of the card-playing world; his concluding exclamation *J'aurais voulu l'embrasser, ce gentilhomme!* ("I wanted to hug him, this aristocrat!") must have

---

[3]   Nevill 136

resonated with his audience because the young yokel has been saved from La Faucheuse ("the mower") — baccarat.

For equal time we consider Nevill on the subject of gambling women.

> When a woman really grasps the spirit of play she is undoubtedly far cleverer than a man, who more often than not regards the gambling as a personal combat between himself and the bank, which he thinks of rather as a living thing than the ruthless inanimate machine which, in sober fact, it is… The majority of women, however, are quite hopeless as gamblers, merely frittering their money away, often quite ignorant of the odds, chances, and general procedure of either trente-et-quarante or roulette, at which their favourite method of staking is to try and back winning numbers.[4]

But back to the big picture:

> At French watering-places gaming flourishes as merrily as ever during the season.   At Trouville, Biarritz, and Aix-les-Bains the game of baccarat forms one of the chief attractions.   There is a good deal of high play at Trouville at the time of the races.   During the present year one player alone — a very rich gambler fond of high stakes — lost no less than a million francs.[5]

The pleasure-loving Edward, Prince of Wales was another rich and famous devotee of baccarat; the game took its toll on high and low, however.

---

[4] Nevill 259
[5] Nevill 134

> So great, indeed, has been the havoc wrought by this game that the French have given it the name of "La Faucheuse," — "the mowing-machine"![6]

Lily Bart is certainly *mowed* financially by cards, bridge in her case, but despite the pity that her decline elicits from the reader, the author seems to have been unmoved by the ruin she had depicted: after *HoM* was finished, the Whartons went to Europe — and Monte Carlo.[7]

Did Edith Wharton herself gamble?   There is no testimony from the biographers (neither Lewis, Benstock, Lubbock, Wright, Wolf, nor Wharton herself), and the inferential evidence is equivocal.   On the negative side, Wharton (or Lily, for that matter) does not fit the real-world profile of the problem gambler, as will be illustrated presently by references to the literature in that field; this suggests that Wharton was working from hearsay.   On the question of this particular episode, we are told that "Edith and Teddy whiled away the hours playing Ping-Pong in the [Monte Carlo] hotel game room."[8]   On the affirmative side, there is the fact that she went to *Monte Carlo*, and at a time when, as Nevill will later inform us, the casino had seen better days, when it was without the patina of gentility that it would later reacquire; in the early 1900's it was as raw and crass as Las Vegas.   In any case, gambling was the only entertainment there.

> Many years before the tables at the German resorts were closed by the Prussian government, M. Blanc [the founder of the casino] was quietly seeking for a suitable spot where his roulette wheels might whirl free from interference and his croupiers deal in unmolested peace.
>
> Gaming-house proprietors seem in one respect to resemble the monks of old, for almost invariably their establishments have

---

[6]   Nevill 313
[7]   Nevill 329
[8]   Lewis 129

been pitched amidst attractive surroundings commanding lovely views. Thoroughly imbued with this tradition, M. Blanc eventually selected the little Principality of Monaco as being a suitable spot to afford his industry a peaceful and alluring haven. After certain negotiations with the reigning Prince Charles Albert, he obtained the required concession, and a Casino (in its earliest days called the "Elysium Alberti") was erected upon the rocky ground known as the Plateau des Spelugues, which, adversaries of gaming will rejoice to learn, means in Monegasque patois "the plain of the robbers."[9]

Adversaries of gaming, on the other hand, were doubtless chagrined at the quality of the robbed, who were a Who's Who of the rich and famous of that day.

From about 1882 to 1890 was perhaps the best day of Principality from a social point of view, for at that time it was the resort of a number of the most distinguished and fashionable people in Europe. All the sporting characters of the day made a point of paying a yearly visit to Monte Carlo...[10]

Whatever Wharton's personal involvement may have been, her mention of gambling and Monte Carlo in *HoM* gave her book the vicarious topicality that follows the Beautiful People. Another sort of topicality may be inferred from Nevill's passing reference to the "adversaries of gaming." Opposition to games of chance was fierce in Wharton's day, and it took two forms: antagonism toward the pastime itself and a generalized antagonism toward anything that resembled it, especially financial speculation. Since there was more heat than light on the issue, the partisans' view of economics lacked

---

[9] Nevill 319
[10] Nevill 319

clarity: the differences between speculation versus investment, or between venture capital versus old money were all blurred.   Since risk-taking — the freedom to fail, as the late Senator Barry Goldwater put it — is at the heart of the American entrepreneurial system, the equation of any and all risk with any and all forms of gambling, drew the lightning.   Utopianism was in the air, as witness the influence of the Populist and Progressive movements, and dreamers everywhere were preparing for one form or another of heaven on earth; step one was to discredit the status quo, and Wharton's portrayal of what we would now call the Jet Set as dissolute, wastrel gamblers found an avid readership, prepared to believe the worst, which brings us to the second window on the times, involving the "anti's."

Ann Fabian documents the connection that many of Wharton's contemporaries made between gambling and wealth acquired through speculation.   An instructive example is John Philip Quin, a reformed gambler turned lecturer, and author of *19th Century Black Art: or, Gambling Exposed.*

> Like most gambling reformers, Quin attacked the hypocrisy of those in power whose earnings had the least taint of speculation and tried to explain that professional speculators, like professional gamblers, merely dangled pretenses of luck and risk before gullible victims.[11]

Fabian gives vivid illustrations of the Wharton-era paradox of gamblers being execrated while speculators were respectable.   The gambler was something of a pariah, yet he was no different from the heartless operator who deliberates long and earnestly how he may most speedily and surely accomplish the ruin of the man for whom he professes the sincerest friendship.[12]

---

[11]   Fabian 176
[12]   Fabian 177

Quin used his own career to equate the men who operated on the Chicago Board of Trade with the crooked carny gamblers who wandered through the Midwest.   He invoked the moral logic of producerism, explaining that in gamblers' slang the

"man who plays against the gambler is called a 'producer,' and what can that mean but fool or victim?"[13]

Indeed, Quin knew it meant far more.   The equation of producers with suckers signified a shattering change to the morals of the market.[14]

The House of Mirth was Edith Wharton's third title for her novel.[15]   The first was *A Moment's Ornament*, which was a good one: the book focused on the heroine, and the title would seem to have done the same; the one that replaced it, *The Year of the Rose*, was also good, since it particularized the image: the abstract "ornament" became a concrete "rose," again evoking Lily's beauty and its transitoriness.   It was not until late in the composition of the novel that Wharton adopted the present title.   (I would guess that this change was made when the author decided on Simon *Rose*-dale as the name of one of the secondary characters, to avoid confusion.)   To the reader a century after its appearance the last change seems hard to justify: it removed the focus from Lily; there is no important *house* (unless one takes "house " as a synonym for "casino," as in "house rules," which I reject as procrustean); and none of the book's characters has any *mirth* at all.   Explaining the change by a reference to Ecclesiastes is unsatisfactory, since it answers none of the questions above.   A case has been made for the title originating from newspaper coverage of a sensational insurance scandal,[16] but this may be putting the cart before the horse: the timeline is hard to square.   True, *HoM*

---

[13] Fabian 150
[14] Fabian 176
[15] Lewis 134
[16] Westerbrook 134

was published in book form late in 1905, when press coverage of the scandal was at high tide, but it had been published serially in *Scribner's Magazine* beginning in January of that year.   I regard the question of primacy as unresolved ("even money," as the gamblers would say), but either way the scandal is part of the story, if only because it was, at the very least, the source of a great deal of free publicity; it is also a gauge of what the public thought of High Society, and is therefore worth consideration as background.

The "House of Mirth" scandal revealed shady dealings that extended as far as the U.S. Senate, but it began simply enough.   The founder of the Equitable Life Assurance Society had died in 1899, and control of the company's assets, a four-hundred-million-dollar "kitty," passed to a son who proved to be a worthless playboy.   Long-time investors rebelled, and backed another son, equally fatuous, but more malleable; J.P. Morgan and others supported the first.   Press coverage of the fight turned up millions in "slush funds" and bogus loans to cronies, state legislators, judges, and a U.S. senator.   One Andrew Fields was the company's chief lobbyist, and his headquarters in Albany, from which he directed lobbying efforts that favored the company, was a residence which the papers dubbed "the House of Mirth."   Although today's reader can admire *HoM* without knowing this, it is interesting to note how Wharton's title resonated with its original audience.

The combination of the widespread revulsion against gambling, on one hand, and the indignation against the corrupt rich that the insurance scandal created, on the other, brought up a third resentment, the widespread view that Wall Street speculators were no better than card sharps, which appealed to the public's ongoing fascination with the rich and famous, particularly when it afforded a glimpse of their private lives.   Wharton's appeal to these strong social currents paid off: *HoM* was a great success.

Ten days after publication [her editor] notified Edith Wharton gravely that "so far we have not sold many over 30,000, but perhaps that will satisfy your expectations for the first fortnight." ... Over the first two months of 1906, Edith could several times record that *The House of Mirth* was still the best-selling novel across the country...[17]

Here it may be pointed out that Wharton's circle represented sedate, genteel old money as opposed to brash, energetic new, and this distinction is worth some comment. First, in some quarters the mention of the rich and famous triggers rage regardless of such nuances, as witness Marie Bristol's astonishingly vitriolic article on *HoM* in the normally sedate, genteel *Western Humanities Review*.[18] The rich are the "parasite class;" Henry James was a "dried-up old virgin who never did anything more strenuous than lift an oyster fork..." Bristol is worth citing to establish a leftward limit of interpretation, but she is by no means alone in her Union Maid stridency. We may take it, however, that the rest of Wharton's readership was conscious of the difference between old money and new, and in any case *HoM* has both kinds of characters.

Gambling differentiates the two. The gracious old money goes to Monte Carlo and plays bridge for money, to while away the hours; the personification of new money, Rosedale, does not. Yet it is to be reiterated that the author herself was a personification of the old. Similarities between Wharton's set and the characters in *HoM* are also to be noted, beginning with the author herself: Wharton, like Lily Bart, was "a 'lady' out of a time and world when the word meant absolute indifference" to commercial matters.[19] Even the men of Wharton's world, like the male characters in *HoM*, exemplified the easy ways of old money, and were not vitally involved in business development or expansion. For the men and women of her world, in Yeats's phrase, "all's accustomed, ceremonious." Yet this very

---

[17] Lewis 151
[18] Bristol 371
[19] Bell 295

staidness makes them restless.   Again, the worldly-wise Nevill: "As a matter of fact the strongest motive with all mankind, after the more sordid necessities are provided for, is excitement.   For this reason gambling will continue — even should all card-playing be declared illegal and all race-courses ploughed up."[20]

There are two *HoM* characters who are not in this pleasant rut: Simon Rosedale and Nettie Struthers.   It is stretching a point to call them gamblers, but there is a sense in which they can be called risk-takers: they are climbers.

Nettie refuses to stay down, and however modest her triumph may seem, it has involved taking chances, on getting a new kind of job, marrying, and having a baby, all enterprises where things can go wrong.   Here the insight of Louise K. Barnette is useful, that Nettie is the only character in *HoM* who escapes commodification, which for Barnette is the striking thing about *HoM*.   With the other characters, "every encounter can be translated into material terms, however trivial," she states.[21]   Commodification is her key to understanding *HoM*, and her points are well taken; money is constantly in the background, whether from games of chance, from speculation, from a future husband or from an inheritance.   Nettie has achieved the intangibles.

Rosedale does not escape commodification, but only because he is a commodifier.   Wharton describes him as having small sidelong eyes which gave him the air of appraising people as if they were bric-a-brac.

The intangible that he pursues is more elusive than Nettie's: he wants status. Understanding Rosedale is elusive for the reader, because it is not clear how much stock one can put in the clues Wharton gives. "Rosedale" seems an obvious Anglicization of "Rosenthal" (the "Rose-" and "Rosen-" elements being cognate; a טאָל ["tal"] in Yiddish is a valley or *dale*), and the name Rosenthal is a 100% pure Ashkenazic, that is, European Jewish name.   This is only a clue,

---

[20]   Nevill 434
[21]   Barnett 54

however, if Wharton was aware of the nuance, which would only have been possible if her anti-Jewish contempt had been bred from familiarity. Did she even know of the difference between Ashkenazim and Sephardim? The Jews themselves certainly did (and do): the Sephardic Jews of New York were Old Money, pre-American Revolution families of Spanish origin (whose saga is admirably recounted in Stephen Birmingham's *The Grandees*), who were embarrassed by their impoverished, recently-arrived Yiddish-speaking kinsmen, the Ashkenazic Jews from Poland and Lithuania. Since there is no mention of Rosedale being an immigrant, he would seem to be a German Jew, one of whose forebears had arrived in-between. Irene Goldman's essay[22] is worth noting at this point; she proceeds from the premise that Rosedale is nowhere explicitly identified as a Jew, but that Wharton implies this by stereotypes. This is wrong: a computer scan reveals that "Jewish" is used once to describe Rosedale, "Jew" twice in *HoM*. Yet his ethnic identification notwithstanding, it is of no greater importance than his role as a "crasher," a New Money man, and a representative of the gambler-speculator. He is a social climber.

> Mr. Rosedale was still at a stage in his social ascent when it was of importance to produce such impressions.

Above all, his is active, a doer.

> Rosedale, in particular, was said to have doubled his fortune, and there was talk of his buying the newly-finished house of one of the victims of the crash… Mr. Rosedale meant to have a less meteoric career. He knew he should have to go slowly, and the instincts of his race fitted him to suffer rebuffs and put up with delays.

---

[22] Goldman 25

Today he might be portrayed as a Texas oilman or a Japanese electronics tycoon.

Having dealt with two of the minor characters, it is time to consider the heroine: in what sense is Lily Bart a gambler?

> For a long time she had refused to play bridge. She knew she could not afford it, and she was afraid of acquiring so expensive a taste. She had seen the danger exemplified in more than one of her associates…

Lily's lavish "social whirl" is also a whirlpool, to use Helen Killoran's phrase;[23] she also proposes as a precursor of *HoM* (via structural allusion) the 1897 novel *The Whirlpool* by George Gissing, which focuses on the theme of financial excess. Excess is the important word.

> …in the last year she had found that her hostesses expected her to take a place at the card-table. It was one of the taxes she had to pay for their prolonged hospitality, and for the dresses and trinkets which occasionally replenished her insufficient wardrobe. And since she had played regularly the passion had grown on her.

I quibble with the last sentence, because it does not ring true with the picture that emerges form a survey of the literature of gambling addiction, which I cite with hesitation. *Caveat lector*! The ground is shaky here: the reader will discover that, in addition to being *a priori* an inexact science, the nuts and bolts of the study of problem gambling involve wide cultural variables and flawed methodology. As an example of the latter problem, it is a standard working hypothesis in that field to proceed on the analogy of alcoholism, and to appropriate data from that literature. *Caveat lector*! As an example

---

[23] Killoran 96

of the sociological variables, the *Queen of Hearts* project, which is specifically about women with gambling problems, has very interesting data; this study, however, was done in the 1990's, in Australia, and with women whose composite profile in no way resembles either Lily Bart or Edith Wharton.   On the important question of gambling and suicide, the experts are blandly ambiguous.[24] *Caveat lector*!

With full knowledge of just how thin the ice is, we proceed. Wharton says that "the passion [for gambling] had grown on her;" but is this assertion borne out in the novel?   Is Lily hooked?   No, according to the literature.   The gambling addict typically gets money for gambling by cutting back on luxuries;[25] does Lily?   Not a chance: she cuts back on bridge to keep herself as comfortable as possible. Does Lily find that gambling brightens up her uneventful life?[26]   Not at all: it is a "tax."   We read in the specialized literature that the problem gambler goes through four phases: [27]   winning, losing/chasing one's losses, desperation, and hopelessness.   Lily quits as soon as she starts losing.   Does Wharton portray her heroine as having predisposing factors like a history of "luck" games like lotteries or bingo?   Are all of Lily's previous "coping skills...abandoned for the anesthetizing quality that gambling has for [her]?"   Is it her "only coping mechanism?"[28]   Lily keeps her poise to the end.

> One of Lily's genuine virtues is that she never fully loses her naiveté, never completely corrupts the artistic finish of her nature.[29]

---

[24] "Suicide" 1

[25] Brown and Coventry Pt. 1, p.2

[26] Brown and Coventry Pt. 4, p.2

[27] Women Gamblers 1

[28] Women Gamblers 4

[29] Wolf 117

Our survey of the question comes to a close with a comment on Lily's death.

> Finally, in her room, Lily is exhausted, but victorious over her temptation to blackmail the enemy who has destroyed her reputation.   How she uses almost all of a small legacy that has just arrived from her aunt's estate to pay her other destroyer, Gus Trenor.   It is a silent and lonely victory and her heroism will never be recognized or praised.   Having no money left for food or medicine, Lily in a confused condition takes an overdose of chloral even as she thinks of facing the next day (A final gamble!)[30]

This is the vanishing point of our investigation: it is well to consider gambling in its literal sense, and in the related senses that Wharton's first readers understood it, but for the figurative senses, such as Lily's "gambling" that her beauty will last, or "gambling" that she will be able to land a rich husband, the tools of library research and literary analysis are too crude: we must leave them at the threshold of *The House of Mirth* itself, and rely instead on careful reading and reflection.

---

[30] McDowell 23

Chaucer the Alchemist

It May seem paradoxical to assert that *The Second Nun's Tale* and *The Canon's Yeoman's Tale* are companion pieces: the former, after all, is a meticulous translation of a saint's life, a foursquare one, with not a trace of ambiguity or irony, while the latter is a sordid tale of swindling. On the face of it, it is *The Prioress's Tale* that most resembles *The Second Nun's Tale*: both are saints' lives, both have invocations of Mary that derive from Dante, both are rhyme royal, and both involve Christians who get their throats cut by unbelievers, yet live on. The grounds for considering *The Canon's Yeoman's Tale* as the companion piece are usually metaphorical or figurative:

> Transformation – an alteration in substance or appearance – ... yokes together in an uneasy narrative partnership tales about a saint and an alchemist: a record of supernatural miracles on the one hand and of a successful confidence game on the other.[1]

I suggest that the relationship between *The Second Nun's Tale* and *The Canon's Yeoman's Tale* is in fact very close: that the former inspired the latter. I propose the following sequence of events: first, that Chaucer composed the St. Cecilia material; next, an intervening episode transpired in which the poet became intimately acquainted with alchemy, either from intellectual curiosity or – more probably – from being bamboozled; and finally, that a sadder but wiser Chaucer

---

[1] Longsworth 87

took a second look at *The Second Nun's Tale*, and saw that it contained the raw material for a tale of alchemy, mutatis mutandis – or rather, transmutatis transmutandis – and *The Canon's Yeoman's Tale* was the result.

Phase I: The Invocacio and the Story of St. Cecilia

Mary Giffin has made a plausible case for *The Second Nun's Tale's* being occasioned by Adam Easton's assumption of the post of Cardinal Priest of Santa Cecilia in Trastevere, which occurred in 1383.[2] I accept this without question, adding only that Chaucer was probably amused at the idea of a *translacion* from the Latin to commemorate the *translacion* of Easton to Italy.

The poet's guiding principle seems to have been replication: the church was dedicated to St. Cecilia, and so was the story; the tale's pope is Urban, and so was the pope of Chaucer's day, albeit the Sixth instead of the First.   For context, we note that both men had difficult papacies.

The first Urban had to deal with Roman persecution; the sixth presided over the Great Schism, and the election of the first anti-pope. England supported Urban, and Chaucer evidently agreed in his heart of hearts, as he departed from his Latin source to insert "*O Cristendom*" for the original "*una [sic] baptisma.*"[3]

Hirsch's point is worth spelling out: in his source Chaucer found *Vnus dominus, una fides, unum baptisma, unus deus et pater omnium.* ("One Lord, one faith, one baptism, one God and father of all...")[4] and rendered it

> *O Lord, o feith, o God, withouten mo,*
> *O Cristendom, and Fader of alle also...*   *208.*

---

[2]   Giffin 29
[3]   Hirsch 129
[4]   Gerould 672

Rather than focus on the one divergence, I would urge attention to the fidelity of the rest of the passage, which is representative of the exactness of the translation for the work as a whole. Every important detail in the narrative, and indeed almost every sentence, is paralleled in the Latin versions of the Cecilia legend.[5]

Chaucer's rendering of the Latin originals, the hagiographic anthology titled *Legenda Aurea* ("Golden Legend") and a *Passio* by Mombritius, is much tighter than, for instance, in his *Boece*. Another example:

> *Et ecce subito apparuit senex quidam niveis vestibus indutus, tenens librum aureis litteris scriptum.*
>
> ("And lo, suddenly a certain old man appeared, dressed in white, having a book inscribed with golden letters.")

Chaucer's versification is literal:

> *And with that word anon ther gan appeere*   *200*
> *An oold man, clad in white clothes cleere,*
> *That hadde a book with lettre of gold in honde,*
> *And gan bifore Valerian to stonde.*

Valerian, of course, is Cecilia's husband. Without going into details, suffice it to say that not only does Chaucer follow the details of the *Legenda Aurea* account, but also the structure (there is a prelude on the etymology of "Cecilia," after which the tale is told), and tone ("Characters do not so much speak as declaim, and dialogue and narrative consist regularly of moral maxims, exclamations, outbursts, and prayers."[6])

Chaucer's translacion is close, but stops short of being slavish: in the Latin sources both Valerian and his brother Tiburce have

---

[5] Reames, "Sources" 111
[6] Brody 118

dramatic courtroom scenes; Chaucer cuts them, thereby highlighting Cecilia's contempt of court.

Phase II: Initiation into Alchemy

Chaucer's complaints about alchemy notwithstanding, he had been warned. The only alchemist mentioned in Dante's *Divine Comedy* is deep in Hell (*Inferno* XXIX, ll. 133-39). Petrarch's dialogue *De Alchimia* has the following exchange:

> *Spes.   Spero Alchimiae successum.*
> *Ratio.   Et quem, quaeso, praeter fumum, cinerem, sudorem, suspiria, verba, dolos, ignominiam?   Hi sunt enim Alchimiæ successus...*
> ("Hope: I hope for alchemy's results.
> Reason: And what, I ask, [might they be] beyond smoke, ashes, sweat, panting, words, sorrow, humiliation?   These are the results of alchemy...")

John Gower writes (*Confessio Amantis IV*)

> *To gete a pound thei spenden fyve;   2591.*
> *I not hou such a craft schal thrive*
> *In the manere as it is used:*
> *It were betre be refused....*

Chaucer must have gone in deep, however, as we gather from his citations of alchemistic literature in *The Canon's Yeoman's Tale*, beginning with the *Rosarie of Arnold of the Newe Toun*, an obvious reference to Arnald of Villa Nova.[7]   Arnald (c.1240-1311) was a Catalonian, but studied medicine at Naples (originally Greek Neapolis, "new town" from ΝΕΑ, "*new, nova,*" ΠΟΛΙΣ, "*town, villa*").   The

---

[7]   Roberts 35

majority of his writings are in fact medical, but his *Rosarius philosophorum* ("Philosophers' Rosary") was famous enough to inspire many imitation "Rosaries" of alchemy. Chaucer knows of the Rosarius (he mentions it by name in line 1429), but shows the depth of his familiarity with the subject by the fact that the passage that he quotes is not from the *Rosarius* at all,[8] but from Arnald's *De Lapide philosophorum* ("Concerning the Philosophers' Stone"), a lesser-known work. His intimacy with this opus may be gathered from the comparison of Arnald

> *quatuor sunt spiritus: sal armonicus: sulphur: arcenicum: argentum vivum:..*
> ("There are four spirits: armoniac salt, sulphur, arsenic, quicksilver...")

with Chaucer's Yeoman's

> *The firste spirit quyksilver called is,*
> *The second orpyment, the thridde, ywis,*
> *Sal armonyak, and the ferthe brymstoon.*   *824.*

(Orpyment, according to the Oxford English Dictionary, is arsenic trisulfide, a yellow compound [*aurum* {"gold"} and "pigment"]; red orpyment was arsenic disulfide, although Chaucer here prefers the more technical term *resalgar*.)

When the poet has the Yeoman prescribe

> *Unslekked lym, chalk, and gleyre of an ey...*   *806.*

He does not mention his source by name, but egg whites are a feature of prescriptions of "Moses."[9] Which Moses? Surely not *the* Moses!

---

[8]   Roberts 37
[9]   Patai 32

The alchemists regarded this as an open question, as distinct from our twenty-first century skepticism: Adam, for example, was not only considered the First Ancestor, but was also cited as the first alchemist,[10] followed by Noah, Solomon, Daniel and other Biblical figures.   Yet there is a way to single "Moses" out: he is the Moses with *the sister*, of whom more later.

The line

As in his book Senior wol bere witnesse,   1450.

shows that Chaucer knew the work of Muhammad ibn Umail, also known as al-Hakim, "the sage."[11]   (He was known to Europe as Senior ["the elder"], the author of the work known by its Latin title *Tabula chemica*.)

Phase III: The Transmutation

Although we can never know the nature and extent of Chaucer's experience with alchemy, we can observe that he presents that science (which is nothing more than proto-chemistry) not as a way to enlightenment, but as a hustle.   Regardless of the unknowables of Chaucer's creative process, it is safe to say that he could have received inspiration for *The Canon's Yeoman's Tale* from a rereading of *The Second Nun's Tale,* seeing double meanings in that originally unambiguous text.

Me, flemed wrecche, in this desert of galle   58.

now reminds him of the bull's gall in the alchemist's witches' brew. The Yeoman would later speak of

---

[10] Patai 30
[11] Ruška 310

Watres rubifiyng, and bolles galle,   797.

The mention of Cecilia's husband,

Which that ycleped was Valerian   129.

recalls that valerian is also a herb, as the Yeoman would mention.

And herbes koude I telle eek many oon,
as egremoyne, valerian and lunarie   800.

Rereading the Latin source, the old man with the golden book, the "one Lord, one faith" passage cited earlier, is not so simple now.   The very next sentence runs,

Cumque hoc legisset, dixit ei senior:
("When he had read this, the older man said to him,")

The *senex* ("old man") has become an older man, *senior*, just like the alchemistic worthy Senior mentioned earlier.   Here Chaucer's first version skipped to the *Passio* of Mombritius, and he recalls how Tiburce's instruction and baptism makes him

Parfit in his lernynge, Goddes knyght.   353.

This from

Quem perfectum doctrina sua per septem dies Christo militem consecravit.
("Whom, completed in his instruction in seven days, he dedicated [as] a soldier to Christ.")[12]

---

[12] Gerould 677

Soldier? *Miles* in Latin, which recalls the hocus-pocus of the alchemistic recipe:

> *Est quidam* miles *nobilis, fortis, et preclarus*
> *Notus omni populo, sed non nimis carus,*
> *Praeclaram habens* coniugem, albis *sed indutam*
> *Filis quoque* igneis *naturaliter sed consutam*
> *Et* fratrem *mirabiliter* ignem abhorrentem...[13]
> ("For there is a noble *soldier,* brave and illustrious, known to all the people, but not overly dear, having a lustrous *spouse,* but dressed in *white* threads and sewn together naturally with *fires,* and a *brother* amazingly *afraid of the fire.*" Emphases mine.)

The noble soldier now suggests sword-wielding Valerian, and in alchemy the *miles* is also an alternative for *sol* ("the sun"), or gold; the white spouse, *luna* ("moon"), silver, could just as easily be Cecilia, or, as Chaucer would render it, *faire Cecilie the white* (113), and Tiburce would be the brother who fears the fire, since he worries that if Pope Urban should show his face,

> *Men sholde hym brennen in a fyr so rede.*   313.

In the original the "brother" would have been any number of reddish iron compounds referred to as Mars.[14]

Even the name of the villain, Almachius, now looks like a metathesized Alchemius ("alchemist"), and the sentence he passes against Cecilia is now ambiguous, even sacriligious:

> *Tunc iratus Almachius iussit eam ad domum suam reduci,*
> *ibique tota nocte et die iussit in bullente balneo concremari.*

---

[13] Grennen 470
[14] Newman 337

("Then Almachius, angry, ordered her sent back to her home, and there day and night to be burned in a boiling hot sauna.")

Reduci is the passive infinitive meaning "to be sent back," but "reduce" was also a term in alchemy that meant (and in modern chemistry still means) "bring to a metallic state by removing non-metallic impurities." Even more suggestive of alchemy, however, is *in bullente balneo*, since it inevitably would call to mind the *balneum Mariae* (bath of Mary), about which a digression is called for. Although this laboratory implement was high-tech in Chaucer's day, it is nothing more complicated than today's double boiler, in which the ingredients to be heated (whether orpyment or okra) are in an interior chamber, the exterior being in actual contact with the flame. In both modern scientific French and German the term is still used (*bain de Marie* and *Marienbad*). The problem is that the Mary in question is not the mother of Jesus whom Chaucer had invoked, but yet another alchemistic worthy[15] the sister of the "Moses" mentioned earlier, known variously as Mary the Jewess, Mary the Copt and Mary the Prophetess. She loomed large in the literature of alchemy, and would be extolled in a later work as one of the twelve elect heroes of that science.

> *Gente Palaestina Moysis soror, ecce Maria*
> *In Chymico pariter gaudet ovatque choro.*
> *Abdita cognovit lapidis mysteria magni*[16]
> ("Behold Mary, sister of Moses, of the race of Palestine; she rejoices and cheers in the Alchemistic chorus. She knew the hidden mysteries of the great stone...")

Being credited with the invention of various instruments of distillation (which might have prompted the description of the sweaty Canon:

---

[15] Patai 61
[16] Patai 79

His forheed dropped as a stillatorie [580.]), and she was also credited with formulas for producing the philosopher's stone.[17]

The coincidence is remarkable: Almachius says

> *For I kan suffre it as a philosphre;*   490.

and Cecilia's rejoinder uses the word *stoon* three times in one stanza (ll. 500, 501 and 503).   *Philosophre* is used only once in *The Second Nun's Prologue,* and once in her *Tale,* and, as can be seen, in the sense of someone wise and stoic; but in *The Canon's Yeoman's Tale* the word, or *philosophie,* is used no less than eleven times, and every time specifically transmuted into a pejorative reference to alchemy.

---

[17] Patai 79

Ahab and Cellini's Perseus

The introductory description of Ahab in Chapter XXVIII of *Moby-Dick* includes the following vivid simile:

> His whole high, broad form, seemed made of solid bronze, and shaped in an unalterable mould, like Cellini's cast Perseus.

Not only is this more specific than simply saying "like a statue," since it particularizes the image, but there is also a very satisfying precision here. Benvenuto Cellini's description of the casting of this statue in his *Autobiography* (Book II, Chapter 78) has an interesting detail. I use the translation of John Addington Symonds.

> After I had let my statue cool for two whole days, I began to uncover it by slow degrees...until I reached the foot of the right leg on which the statue rests...However, when I reached the end, it appeared that the toes and a little piece above them were unfinished, so that about half the foot was wanting.

The relevance to the "dismasted" Ahab is obvious.

For the record, Melville would not actually set eyes on the *Perseus* until after the publication of *Moby-Dick*.

> While Melville first saw Cellini's *Perseus* on March 24, 1857, at the Uffizi Palace in Florence, the famous statue was already

familiar to him through reproductions in bronze and other materials and through prints.[1]

This has nothing to do with the "casting" episode, however. The real question is whether or not this episode would have been known to Melville and his readers.

In fact, the Florentine sculptor's book had been available in the United States as early as 1812, translated by one Thomas Nugent. It is interesting to note that the translation was dedicated to Sir Joshua Reynolds, and that it was available in Philadelphia, Baltimore and Norfolk. Examination of a microfiche copy reveals that the episode of the missing foot is duly included.[2]

There was an additional reason for this episode to have been part of the aesthetic background of the times: the casting of the *Perseus* is the climax of the final act of Hector Berlioz's opera based on the life of the famous sculptor, *Benvenuto Cellini,* which had premiered on September 10, 1838, in Paris. Berlioz, the student of music history will recall, was known not only for the music he wrote but also for the noise he made. He was the consumate gate-crasher. His musical credentials were thin. Arriving in Paris at the height of the "guitaromania," a craze that was a golden age of guitar playing and composition (about 1810-1840), he was only a mediocre player, and he had only one volume of mediocre song arrangements to his credit. The newspaper was his instrument, and he was a virtuoso, writing reviews and criticism with a flair that attracted attention – and enemies. By the time *Benvenuto Cellini* was ready for production, the battle lines were drawn.

Coverage in the Paris press was very extensive, most critics taking the view that the librettos's verse and dramaturgy were trivial and that Berlioz'a music was eccentric and

---

[1] Robillard 81
[2] Nugent 2:177

unmelodic...Mainzer repaid an old score (Berlioz had been severe on his teaching methods in an article two years earlier) with a bitter attack in his *Chronique Musicale*; this appeared on 8 August, before the première, and again in *Le National* on 12 September.[3]

Benvenuto Cellini died by inches, with "sick-outs" by lead singers, backstage bickering and managerial indifference creating headlines at each postponement.[4]   After the fourth performance, on January 11, 1839, the work was declared a flop.   It went staggering on, though: there were further partial performances in Paris (1839); and excerpts were performed in Dresden, Hamburg, Berlin, Hanover and Darmstadt (all in 1843); Vienna (1845); and London (1848).[5]   It would continue to stagger on after the publication of *Moby-Dick,* but its ultimate fate is beyond the scope of this article.   It is enough to say that the brouhaha – we could almost say soap-opera – occasioned by this opera was sufficient to have made it known to Melville's readers, and with it its highlighting of the Perseus episode.

---

[3]   Macdonald xvi
[4]   Macdonald xvi-xvii
[5]   Holoman 180

Two Samuels: Tzara, Beckett and Communism

Václav Havel wrote and signed his "Letter to Dr. Gustav Husák, General Secretary of the Czechoslovak Communist Party" in 1975, at the high water mark of the communist movement. David went to jail, and Goliath appeared no worse for the encounter, although we can now see that the giant had only fifteen more years to live. Although Havel's 1975 "Letter" would cast a very long shadow indeed, for the purposes of this paper I would rather call attention to his 1965 play *The Memorandum*. The trenchant ideas in the "Letter" would provide a blueprint for an enormous political change, but that is a sociological document; *The Memorandum* is an aesthetic one, expressing those ideas in the form of a parable, unforgettable because it is very funny. *The Memorandum* is a marvelous "Prague Spring" satire on the harebrained social tinkering that in its milder forms has been called "the Nanny State," but which can take the form of all-out war against human nature. In *The Memorandum* the sinner is human speech and the savior is *Ptidepe. Ptidepe* is a new official language, artificial, sculpted, designed to banish the confusions of homely, unscientific, natural language. *Ptipede* is engineered based on maximizing the differences between words so that no word can conceivably be mistaken for another. It is engineered for efficiency in that the length of a word is inversely proportional to its frequency of use: the word for wombat, for example, has 319 letters. Alas for the Language Architects, once *Ptidepe* is put in place, it begins to develop, acquiring emotional overtones, ambiguities, in short, some of the characteristics of a natural language, so the Planner/Nannies are back where they started from. They are undaunted, however, and engineer and implement *Chorukor,* a new "designer" language, one based this time on the principle of maximizing the *resemblances* between words. Monday becomes *Ilopagar,* Tuesday *Ilopager;* Tom Stoppard, in the introduction he wrote for the play, wryly suggests that this is so that "the worst that can happen is that the right things will occur on the wrong day of the week."[1]

For perspective, some observations from the peerless Lin Yutang, who interrupted his labors on ancient Chinese philosophy to produce the second-best critique of communism ever written (the best being Havel's "Letter"): "A poet does not analyze; he does not rationalize; he is almost ignorant – happily for him – of polemic clichés and controversial theories. He reaches clarity."[2] I ask the reader to suspend his judgment on the matter of clarity; there is a trump that will validate Lin's position that will turn up shortly, but we must first concern ourselves with two Samuels, Samuels who at first glance would never appear to be exponents of clarity at all. They were similar aesthetically, divergent politically. Both flirted with *Ptidepe.*

The first Samuel is known to literature as Tristan Tzara, but he was born Samuel Rosenstock, on April 16, 1896,[3] an inauspicious year for a francophile Jew: the Dreyfuss Case was reaching its climax, and an anti-semitic hysteria was sweeping France. The hysteria subsided, but the anti-semitism lingered, inseparable from the questions left unresolved by that affair. Young Rosenstock lost no time in losing his Yiddish name for a snappy pseudonym, this in 1915, at the tender age of nineteen,[4] and advertizing himself as Rumanian rather than Jewish, this in Geneva, before crossing the threshold into France, as it were. This is logical. In Sholem Aleichem's *Menachem Mendel* the regular reply to "How are you?" is "How does a Jew do?" The choices were stark: a hard life in obscurity or an

---

[1]   Havel 280
[2]   Lin 4
[3]   Tzara 16
[4]   Tzara 16

exhilarating life at the pinnacle of society (usually via the fine arts or the sciences), both of which were closed to Tzara because, to put it bluntly, he was not a first-rate talent. There was a third way, however. The reader may take his choice of two Yiddish words to describe the profession that Tzara chose: לץ ("letz") or טומלער ("tumler"). The former is literally "mocker," the second, "noisemaker;" in sharper focus, a לץ is a snide, ineffectual sort of gadfly, while a טומלער is a buffoonish pest. Tristan Tzara was a public nuisance in Paris until his death in 1963.

No biographical commentary is required for the other Samuel, Samuel Beckett, except as relates to Tzara and politics. Beckett was in Paris in 1928-29, and knew the latest doings of Tzara and his circle.[5] Back in Dublin in 1931 he produced some Tristan Tzara translations,[6] and he received encouragement from Tzara, who read *Molloy* and admired it greatly.[7]

Before focussing on the ultimately divergent political views of the two Samuels, let us concentrate on their aesthetic ideas.

Literary criticism normally begins with careful reading; in the case of Samuel Beckett's *En Attendant Godot,* however, scrutiny of the text reveals that scrutiny of the text is useless. Exhibit A:

> VLADIMIR: this is not boring you, I hope – how is it that of the four Evangelists only one speaks of a thief being saved. The four of them were there – or thereabouts – and only one speaks of a thief being saved. (*Pause.*) Come on, Gogo, return the ball, can't you, once in a way?
>
> ESTRAGON: (*with exaggerated enthusiasm*). I find this really most extraordinarily interesting.

---

[5] Knowlson 113
[6] Knowlson 137
[7] Knowlson 341

This from the first act of the English version; *Godot,* however, was written in French.   The original version has an attractive bit of counterpoint (which I have marked by arrows) that the English lacks.

> VLADIMIR.—Je ne t'ennuie pas, j'espère.
> ESTRAGON.—Je n'écoute pas. ←
> VLADIMIR.— Comment se fait-il que des quatre évangélistes un seul présent les faits de cette façon?   Ils etaient cependant là tous les quatre – enfin, pas loin. Et un seul parle d'un larron de sauvé.   (*Un temps.*)   Voyons, Gogo, il faut me renvoyer la balle de temps en temps.
> ESTRAGON.—J'écoute. ←

("VLADIMIR: I'm not boring you, I hope. / ESTRAGON: I'm not listening. ← / VLADIMIR: How is it that of the four Evangelists only one tells what happened in this way?   All four of them were there, after all – not far off, at any rate. And just one speaks of a thief getting saved.   (*pause*)   Come on, Gogo, you've got to meet me halfway once in a while. / ESTRAGON: I'm listening. ←")

One assumes as a matter of course that anomalies of this sort are meaningful, especially when the author is known to have had a hand in the editing.   One assumes that if something is left out, or if it is shown to be interchangeable with a different version, that it is because it is not important.   Exhibit B:

> POZZO: True.   (*He sits down.   To Estragon.*)   What is your name?
> ESTRAGON: Adam.

Before being swept up in learnèd rhapsodies over the subtleties and nuances of "Adam," however, a glance at the original.

POZZO.— C'est vrai. (*Il se rassied. A Estragon.*) Comment vous appelez-vous?
ESTRAGON (*du tic au tac*).— Catulle.
("POZZO: That's true. [*He sits again. To Estragon.*] What's your name? / ESTRAGON: [*Quick as a flash*] Catullus.")

Any number of omissions and substitutions could be offered to show that the text of *Godot* is not its primary parameter, and that analysis based on its text is a wild goose chase. Everyone in the audience must have grasped this: the effect of the play depends far more on the actor's horseplay than hairsplitting over whether "Adam" is more forceful than "Catullus." Does this mean that the play is unanalyzable? No: although scrutiny of the text leads nowhere, an examination of *Godot*'s antecedents will show that it's not such a hard nut to crack after all. *Reculons,* as the French say, *pour mieux sauter*: let us back up in order to leap further.

Future French *littérateurs* will doubtless be struck by the fact that not one of their three most notable avant-garde writers of the twentieth century was French. The aforementioned לץ and creator of Dadaism, Tristan Tzara, was a Rumanian Jew; Eugène Ionesco (1912-1994) was Rumanian, although much of his childhood was spent in Paris; and the aforementioned Samuel Beckett (1906-1989) was Irish. By itself, writing and achieving fame in a foreign language is nothing new: Plautus did it two thousand years ago (his first language was not Latin, but Umbrian). In English, one thinks of Joseph Conrad and Ayn Rand, whose first languages were Polish and Russian, respectively. Yet it is important to note that while foreign writers in English have been serious and respectful of the literary continuum, the "guest-writers" in France have consistently bitten the hand that fed them, producing works that are little more than attention-getting pranks.

dododo
immense panse pense et pense pense
Erdera Vendrell
endran drandre
rendre prendre entre rendre rendre prendre prendre

The above is from Tzara's *La première Aventure céleste de M. Antipyrine* ("The First Celestial Adventure of Mr. Tylenol," since, as Elmer Peterson informs us, Antipyrine was a popular headache remedy in France and Switzerland in 1916, when the play was produced in Zurich).[8]   Peterson also notes that there are no page numbers or division into acts and scenes in this play,[9] which makes citation impossible; more importantly, he draws attention to the names of Tzara's characters.   "Infantile names like BleuBleu, CriCri, and PiPi have a contemporary progeny in Samuel Beckett's Gogo and Didi in *Waiting for Godot*."[10]

Another Tzara touch is the attractive bits of sound-play.
> VLADIMIR.--...Il saigne!
> POZZO.—C'est bon signe.
> ("VLADIMIR: It's bleeding! / POZZO. – That's a good sign.")

Pozzo later intones

> Godet...Godot...Godin

both of which are more elegant than the rumble-bumble of Tzara's *rendre-prendre* above.
Rumble-bumble, however, was *de rigueur* in this little corner of the French stage.   Even Ionesco, in *Rhinocéros,* his passionate,

---

8   Peterson 6
9   Peterson 227
10   Peterson 10

heartfelt Jeremiad about The Bad Guys (I can be no more specific, since the Left claims that the play is about a Rightist takeover, while the Right alleges that it is about a Leftist takeover), even as the suspense is building, in Act II, can't resist having a character begin with the jangling *Vous avez vu, vous...* which, for all its preposterousness in French, is nothing more than "You have seen, you..."   The audience expected it.   It was conventional.

For a different Dadaism, consider the deadening repetition of *demande* in the following snippet.

> VLADIMIR.— Tu peux lui demander maintenant.   Il est
>   alerté.
> ESTRAGON.—Lui demander quoi?
> VLADIMIR.—Pourquoi il ne dépose pas ses bagages.
> ESTRAGON.—Je me le demande.
> ("VLADIMIR: You can ask him now.   He's on alert. /
> ESTRAGON: Ask him what?
> VLADIMIR: Why he doesn't put his baggage down. /
> ESTRAGON: I wonder about that.")

The Parisian audience of 1952 must have been in heaven.   The *après guerre* grayness had been dispelled by this ragbag of old, pre-war clichés that Beckett had assembled.   *Vive Godot!*

The more attentive Parisians might have noted, however, that Beckett was worlds away from Tzara in terms of dialogue: Beckett's exchanges are propelled by non-sequiturs; Tzara avoids non-sequiturs, sequiturs, any kind of connection between words.   He gives a recipe.

Pour Faire un poème dadaiste

> Prenez un journal
> Prenez des ciseaux
> Choisissez dans ce journal un article ayant la longueur
> que vous comptez donner à votre poème.

Découpez l'article.

Découpez ensuite avec soin chacun des mots que forment cet article et mettez-les dans un sac.

Agitez doucement.

Sortez ensuite chaque coupure l'une après l'autre.

Copiez consciencieusement

dans l'ordre où elles ont quitté le sac.

Le poème vous ressemblera.

Et vous voilà un écrivain infiniment original et d'une sensibilité charmante, encore qu'incomprise du vulgaire.[11]

("Take a newspaper / Take a pair of scissors / Choose in the newspaper an article having the length / that you want your poem to have.   / Cut the article out. / Then carefully cut out each of the words that form / that article and put them in a sack. / Shake gently. / Then take each cutting, one after the other. / Copy conscientiously / in the order in which they have left the sack / The poem will resemble you. / And there you will be, an infinitely original writer and of a / charming disposition, although still misunderstood / by the common herd.")

This is flim-flam, of course.   Tristan Tzara, as should be evident from the above quotations, was not especially talented; the emperor was naked, although flamboyantly naked.   When Dadaism ceased to draw a crowd, he underwent a well-publicized conversion to surrealism; when that played out, he moved to a stagy Marxism.   The French speak of *l'éternel devenir,* "always becoming," with the nuance of never arriving.   In Yiddish, one speaks of a ליץ or a טומלער.

Beckett was quite the opposite of Tzara in the technical details of his work: his dialogue is sharp, his plot focused.   The two men were opposites as well in the way they carved out their respective niches:

---

[11] Peterson 35

Beckett became famous for *Godot*, not for any self-promoting escapades.   The reader would do well, however, to remember that there is a continuum between the two men in the role they played in Paris, that if no torch was passed to Beckett, Tzara's cap and bells were.

> tristan tzara
> Regardez-moi bien!
> Je suis idiot, je suis un farceur, je suis un fumiste.
> Regardez-moi bien!
> Je suis laid, mon visage n'a pas d'expression, je suis petit.
> Je suis comme vous tous![12]
> ("Take a good look at me! / I'm an idiot I'm a joker, I'm a fake. / Take a good look at me! / I'm ugly, my face has no expression, I'm little. / I'm like all of you!)

Thus Beckett's predecessor.   For this discussion, however, whether he was a fake or not is secondary; Tzara is the key to understanding *Godot*, or more particularly how this tiresome, tacky piece became world famous.

Godot began a new phase in Beckett's life; it is time to deal with a new phase in Tzara's: communism.   *Reculons pour mieux sauter.* The earlier mention of Tzara's arrival in Geneva in 1915 may have piqued the reader's curiosity as to a more famous visitor to that city who had arrived some time before, Vladimir Ilych Lenin, whose address at number 6 Spiegelgasse was directly across the street from the Cabaret Voltaire, the mecca of literary young turks in Geneva. There is a story, perhaps apocryphal, to the effect that Lenin and Tzara played chess there.[13]   If true, it would seem that Lenin's persuasive ability made no impression on his young opponent; Tzara later claimed to have been on the side of the 1917 revolution, but if that be true, his

---

[12]   Peterson 33
[13]   Peterson 190

publications at the time were strangely silent on the subject.   Not until 1931 did he begin to gravitate toward Marxism with an essay titled "Essai sur la Situation de la Poésie," where Marx was among the authorities he cited for his developing vision, which would reach its final expression in 1935; then, at the Congrès International des Ecrivains, he announced that he had become a communist,[14] and that he had discovered that "directed thought" was in the service of the bourgeoisie, whereas "undirected thought" was Marxist, and that he was therefore a Marxist, or rather, that he had more or less always been one, or rather, that he could now be a Marxist convert without the necessity of conversion.   The perceptive reader may suspect a shell game; the suspicion is confirmed by Tzara's tour of the Spanish Civil War. Picasso would be moved to paint *Guernica* by that national agony; Tzara emitted nothing more than his usual self-conscious twitter:

> Espagne 1936
> jeunesse des pas dans la cendre
> le soleil dévoile ta matinale surdité
> lorsque le serpent se mêle de labourer
> aux lentes fonderies de cristal...
> ("Spain 1936 / youth of steps in the ashes / the sun unveils your morning deafness / when the serpent takes a hand in plowing / by the slow foundries of crystal...")[15]

and on and on.   The fact that there was a war on, the objective reality of the suffering it was causing, would seem to have been water off a duck's back.   Lenin, who also had a position in the Communist Party, not only opposed Tzara in chess, but also in epistemology (in *Materialism and Empirio-Criticism*):

---

[14] Peterson 118
[15] Peterson 193

From the standpoint of modern materialism, or Marxism, the relative limits of our approximation to the cognition of the objective, absolute truth are historically conditioned; but the existence of this truth is unconditioned, as well as the fact that we are contiually approaching it...In a word, every ideology is historically conditioned, but it is unconditionally true that to every scientific theory (as distinct from religion) there corresponds an objective truth, something absolutely so in nature.[16]

What kind of party did Tzara think he was joining?

Beckett flirted with Marxism about this time,[17] but until writing *Catastrophe,* of which more later,

Beckett sometimes expressed regret that, because of this essentially nondidactic approach to writing, he was unable (and had certainly been unwilling) to write anything that dealt overtly with politics.[18]

Here the reader may protest that this tongue-tiedness contradicts Lin Yutang's statement that the poet gives us clarity, that Beckett and Tzara were conscienceless, self-indulgent peddlers of *Ptidepe.* I answer that this simply proves that at this point Tzara and Beckett were *poseurs.* In 1982 Beckett, a *poseur* no longer, would electrify the world – and shame it – with *Catastrophe.* Tzara would always remain a *poseur,* or a ליץ, or a טומלעֶר, if you will.

Another difference between the two was the fact that Beckett occupied himself with staying sane and fending off adulatory "groupies." (In the index of one biography under "Beckett, Samuel Barclay," there is a subcategory for references to "piercing blue eyes

---

[16] Lenin 13:107
[17] Gordon 100
[18] Knowlson 596

of." I am not making this up.) On the other hand, Tzara was playing with fire, as witness the letters of his old chess opponent, Vladimir Ilych Lenin, which give us the other side of the coin: the tyrant's-eye view of the artist. I find no references to Tzara in the meticulously edited correspondence of Lenin, but the avant-garde Mayakovsky will serve as a stand-in; Beckett's double in this case will be Gorky, who received letters from Lenin that are by turns adulatory, wheedling and bullying. On February 7, 1908 Lenin, in Geneva, wrote to Gorky, on Capri:

> I agree with you a thousand times about the need for *systematically* combating political decadence, renegadism, whining, and so forth. I do not think that there would be any disagreement between us about "society" and the "youth". The significance of the intellectuals in our Party is declining; news comes from all sides that the intelligentsia is *fleeing* the Party. And a good riddance to these scoundrels. The Party is purging itself from petty-bourgeois dross. The workers are having a bigger say in things. The old role of the worker-professionals is increasing. All this is wonderful, and I am sure that your "kicks" must be understood in the same sense...Ah, there is nothing good about all those special, long articles of literary criticism scattered through various semi-Party and non-Party periodicals! We should try to take a step away from this old, intellectualist, stuffed-shirt manner, that is, we should link literary criticism, too, more closely with Party work, with Party leadership.[19]

In a published speech from 1910 Lenin proclaimed, speaking of a rival faction:

---

[19] Lenin 34:379

...They have a certain positive content. This positive content can be expressed in one name: Maxim Gorky...Gorky is undoubtedly the greatest representative of *proletarian* art, one who has done a great deal for this art and is capable of doing still more in the future...In the field of proletarian art Gorky is an enormous asset in spite of his [non-orthodox] sympathies...[20]

Gorky is mentioned, almost reverently, in a letter (February 13, 1908) to A. V. Lunacharsky, later the first education minister of the U.S.S.R. One notes that the ideas are the mirror image of the above.

Your plan for a section of *belles-lettres* in *Proletary* [magazine] and for having A.M. [Gorky] run it is an excellent one, and pleases me exceedingly.   I have in fact been dreaming of making the *literature and criticism* section a permanent feature in *Proletary* [the publication in question] and having A.M. to run it.   But I was *afraid,* terribly afraid of making the proposal outright, as I *do not know* the nature of A. M.'s work (and his work-bent).[21]

Thus Lenin-Jekyll; years later Gorky would receive a letter from Lenin-Hyde, responding (September 15, 1919) to Gorky's protest against a mass incarceration:

Reading your frank opinion on this matter, I recall a remark of yours, which sank into my mind during our talks (in London, on Capri, and afterwards):
"We artists are irresponsible people."
Exactly!   You utter incredibly angry words about what? About a few dozen (or perhaps even a few hundred) Cadet and

---

[20] Lenin 16:207
[21] Lenin 16:383

near-Cadet gentry spending a few days in jail *in order to prevent plots like that of the surrender of Krasnaya Gorka* [a town], plots which threaten the lives of *tens* of thousands of workers and peasants.

A calamity, indeed! What injustice! A few days or even weeks, in jail for intellectuals in order to prevent the massacre of tens of thousands of workers and peasants!

"Artists are irresponsible people."...

No. There is no harm in such "talents" being made to spend some weeks or so in prison.[22]

Lin Yutang's words are worth quoting as a rebuttal: "...one writ of habeas corpus is worth all the Confucian classics."[23]

In 1922 Lenin-Jekyll speaks publicly of the avant-garde:

Yesterday I happened to read in *Izvestia* a political poem by Mayakovsky. I am not an admirer of his poetical talent, although I admit that I am not a competent judge. But I have not for a long time read anything on politics and administration with so much pleasure as I read this. In his poem he derides this meeting habit, and taunts the Communists with incessantly sitting at meetings. I am not sure about the poetry; but as for the politics, I vouch for their absolute correctness. We are indeed in the position, and it must be said that it is a very absurd position, of people sitting endlessly at meetings, setting up commissions and drawing up plans without end.[24]

This followed by a folksy disquisition on Oblomov, the Russian patron saint of indolence. Yet how full of energy is Lenin-Hyde's letter to Lunacharsky (May 6, 1921):

---

[22] Lenin 44:284
[23] Lin 14
[24] Lenin 33:223

> Aren't you ashamed to vote for printing 5,000 copies of Mayakovsky's "150,000,000"?
> It is nonsense, stupidity, double-dyed stupidity and affectation.
> I believe such things should be published one in ten, and *not more than 1,500 copies,* for libraries and cranks.
> As for Lunacharsky, he should be flogged for his futurism.[25]

Later that same day, a note to a party functionary:

> Again and again, I request you to help us fight futurism, etc.
> Lunacharsky has (alas!) got through the collegium the printing of Mayakovsky's "150,000,000".
> Can't we stop this?   It must be stopped.   Let's agree that the futurists are to be published not more than twice a year *and not more than 1,500 copies.*
> They say that Lunacharsky has once again driven out Kiselis, who is reputed to be a *"realist"* artist, while directly and *indirectly* promoting a futurist.
> Could you find some reliable *anti-*futurists?[26]

Evidently, reliable *anti-*futurists were in fact found, many of them: the student of Soviet art must have a high tolerance for pseudo-folksongs (my "favorite" would be «Когда трактор в поле ходит», "When the tractor goes through the fields, [the soul is joyful]"), paintings of Lenin and poems that rhyme relentlessly.   Yet no matter how reliable the *anti-*futurists were, there arose the problem (if the reader will indulge a little Marxist grammar) of anti-*anti-*futurists, which brings us to Beckett's *Catastrophe.*

It is hard to believe that this piece was written by the author of *Godot.*   It is dedicated to Václav Havel, who was in jail for

---

[25] Lenin 45:138
[26] Lenin 45:139

subversion, presumably as an anti-*anti*-futurist. Beckett seized the opportunity to write a play that would demonstrate his solidarity with a victimized, imprisoned fellow writer but could express his own themes and be written in his own manner.   He wasted no time.   He was asked for a contribution early in the year and, although the first manuscript caries no date, the second is dated "20 February 1982."[27] In contrast to *Godot,* the plot of *Catastrophe* is straight as an arrow and in deadly earnest: the Protagonist, humiliated, reduced, "baited" throughout the play, in the end "raises his head, fixes the audience," and reduces their applause to a stunned silence.[28]   A biographer writes that

> Beckett told me that in referring to what one might describe as the "grand finale," a reviewer had claimed that it was "ambiguous."   "There's no ambiguity there at all," he said angrily.   "He's saying: You bastards, you haven't finished me yet!"[29]

Now we have caught up with Lin Yutang's dictum: Beckett does not analyze; he does not rationalize; *Catastrophe* is devoid – happily for it – of polemic clichés and controversial theories; but here Beckett reaches the clarity that Lin was speaking of.   Havel, by the way, was paroled a few months later.

---

[27] Knowlson 596
[28] Knowlson 298
[29] Knowlson 597

Localization

There is nothing new under the sun.   Many years ago I stood in a museum in Colombia, recalling the words of a favorite history professor: "Foreign businessmen came into South America, and instead of giving their companies patriotic-sounding Spanish-language names, they chose names that the people couldn't even pronounce." And there before me was the proof: a stock certificate from many, many years ago, issued in this Spanish-speaking country, with the English name of "The Bogota Telephone Company."   A word or two in a foreign language may be charming, but a document in a foreign language, particularly one touching the reader's liberty, health or money, is not charming at all.

What were they thinking, those men who set up "The Bogota Telephone Company?"   Did they want investors, or didn't they? They obviously brought brains, cash and sweat to the project, or rather to ninety-nine percent of it; but they seem to have given no thought to the final one percent of it, the way that they connected with the customers who would use their telephones, and with the local investors who would risk their money on the enterprise.   Did "The Bogota Telephone Company" have no competitors?   It makes no difference. Did this company have a sweetheart deal with the government, one that guaranteed it monopoly status?   All the more reason to take local sensibilities into account.

Modern terminology would express this situation as globalization versus localization: globalization in the sense that a transnational endeavor was taking place, a company from the Anglosphere operating in South America, as if borders did not exist, and whose product, the telephone, would contribute to further diminishing the limitations of borders; and localization in the negative sense that this company had not done its homework, and instead of capitalizing on its customers' fund of memories and dreams, chose a name that was at best neutral, and at worst an irritant to those customers.

I have no quarrel with the word "globalization," since this new word describes a new reality; in the past, borders were eliminated by conquest.   We must not be limited by the modern sense of the word "localization," however, because using it in a limited way will lead us astray.   It is not the opposite of this new word "globalization," because the reality that "localization" describes is not new at all, being older even than the carelessly-named "Bogota Telephone Company." What we are talking about is not hard to understand; what we in the year 2008 call "localization" is simply the old, old reality of doing business using common sense.

What is close at hand affects me, and I intuitively want to have some influence over it; what is over the horizon is beyond my control, whether it benefits me or not.   This abstract situation requires me to think and act counter-intuitively, which is the opposite of what a business transaction must be.   Did the people of Bogota, Colombia want telephones?   They did.   Why complicate things, then?   "The Bogota Telephone Company" doubtless had strict quality control over its products and services, that first ninety-nine percent of its effort; quality control, however, must be one hundred percent, and must include the intangibles as well.

Experience is the best teacher, goes the proverb, but this is nonsense.   Experience is the worst teacher: experience is harsh, experience can even be devastating.   Someone else's experience is the best teacher, and always has been.   There is nothing new under the sun.

A Case of Modernist Poetic אומפֿארשטענדלעכקייט

Reading Edwin Arlington Robinson not long ago, my eye came to rest on a blemish seldom encountered in the works of that fine poet: it was in "The White Lights (Broadway, 1906)."

> When Flaccus bade Leuconoë
> To banish her Chaldean ways,   (11.11-12)

This is jabberwocky.   Learnèd jabberwocky, perhaps, but still jabberwocky, and especially jarring since it intrudes into an otherwise clear and forceful poem.   I could overlook rhyme-chasing, if that were the cause for Robinson's veering into the fog this way.   What bothered me was not the impenetrability of these lines to readers at the beginning of the de-Latinized twenty-first century, but my suspicion that they had been equally impenetrable to readers at the beginning of the twentieth. The only clue that Robinson gives to identify his source — and therefore his meaning — as the eleventh poem of the first book of Horace's *Odes* is the nonce-name *Leuconoë.* The only reason I recognized the reference was because I had memorized the original some thirty years before, according to the bewhiskered praxis of that bygone era.

> *Tu ne quaesieris – scire nefas – quem mihi, quem tibi*
> *finem di dederint, Leuconoë, nec Babylonios*
> *temptaris numeros.*
> ("Do not seek – to know would be sacrilege – what destiny the gods have alotted to me and you, Leuconoë [a woman's name], nor try Babylonian calculations [astrology])."

This is the *carpe diem* ("seize the day") ode.   Flaccus?   Fie! The only one-named Flaccus in Latinity is the slave who wrote the music for one of Terence's plays.   Quintus Horatius Flaccus was the poet's full name, but for centuries he has been neither "Flaccus" nor "Quintus" but Horace; "Chaldean" for "Babylonian?" Fig leaf on top of fig leaf! For most readers, the reference is a closed book anyway, so further obfuscation is gratuitous, and especially galling considering Robinson's trademark vividness.   O mighty Caesar, dost thou lie so low?

We should go easy on Robinson, however, since, in Seneca's phrase (the reader will indulge one final backward glance at Latinity), *Quae fuerunt vitia, mores sunt* ("What once were vices, now are common behavior").   Robinson's nonce אומפאַרשטעענדלעכקייט became pervasive in the works of modernist poets.

The Pandora in this case was Ezra Pound, who changed the course of English literature when he edited T. S. Eliot's *The Waste Land.* Although Pound's own poetry is now of only period interest, Eliot's poem proved to be seminal: for decades afterward poetry monthlies were freighted with lumbering, footnoted imitations by lesser talents. Pound and Eliot met in London on September 22, 1914, and by August 12 of the following year Pound could write in a letter, "A young chap named Eliot has gone back to America for a bit.   I have more or less discovered him."   It was Pound's "pull" that got *The Love Song of J. Alfred Prufrock* published in *Poetry*.[1]   When Eliot's parents were distressed at his choice of a writing career, he prevailed on Pound to write them a testimonial to the effect that a writer's life is not so bad.[2] Eliot sent the older poet his *Waste Land* for editorial help.   Pound warped the poem; the way he warped the poem mirrors the way he warped his own poetry, from the catty, but lively, topicality of

---

[1]   Eliot, T. S. *The Waste Land: A Facsimile and Transcript of the Original Drafts Including the Annotations of Ezra Pound.* Eliot, Valerie, ed.   Harcourt Brace, Jovanovich, 1971.   Abbreviated as *Facsimile.*   p. ix

[2]   *Letters,* Eliot, T.S.   *The Letters of T. S. Eliot: Volume I 1898-1922..*   Eliot, Valerie, ed.   Harcourt Brace Jovanovich, 1988.   Abbreviated as *Letters.* p. 99.

Mauberly (of period interest) to the gibberish of the *Cantos* (which are, to all intents and purposes, dead and buried).   I suspect, although I cannot prove, that the success of *The Waste Land* excited Pound's hubris, and may have accelerated the process of his own self-marginalization; if so, it would be a sort of poetic justice.

But let us begin at the beginning. I define אומפארשטטענדלעכקייט as words that are not in the reader's vocabulary, not explained in context, and not in the dictionary.   I take it as axiomatic that אומפארשטענדלעכקייט is appropriate to light verse (Who cares what a boojum tree is?) but out of place in an involved piece like *The Waste Land*, where meticulous reading is called for.

It is on the latter point that Pound skewed young Eliot's poem, by cutting parts of the original that were approachable, even folksy, and by introducing words and phrases that were אומפארשטענדלעך. Examination of the original poem shows that Eliot's confection had included generous garnishes of mysogyny, scatology and the "genteel anti-Semitism" of the times.   In the original opening of "The Fire Sermon" the "white-armed Fresca" is served her morning cup

> Of soothing chocolate, or stimulating tea.
> Leaving the bubbling beverage to cool,
> Fresca slips softly to the needful stool,
> Where the pathetic tale of Richardson
> Eases her labour till the deed is done.

Which Richardson? *Pamela?* It hardly matters.   Fresca has breakfast in bed and answers a few letters.

> This ended, to the steaming bath she moves,
> Her tresses fanned by little flutt'ring Loves;
> Odours, confected by the cunning French,
> Disguise the good old hearty female stench.[3]

---

[3] *Facsimile,* p. 23.

No footnotes are required for this! It is noteworthy however, that Eliot's correspondence in these years is full of raunchy rhymes. From 1914:

> *Now* while our heroes were at sea
> They pass'd a German warship.
> The captain pac'd the quarterdeck
> Parading in his corset.
> What ho!   they cry'd, we'll sink your ship!
> And so they up and sink'd her.
> But the cabin boy was sav'd alive
> And bugger'd, in the sphincter.[4]

In 1915 Eliot writes, "I fear that King Bolo and his Big Black Kween will never burst into print."[5]   In 1916 it still had not, but in a letter to Conrad Aiken verses are written out; a sampler:

> King Bolo's big black bassturd kween
> Her taste was kalm and klassic
> And as for anything obscene
> She said it made her ass sick....
> King Bolo's big black bassturd kween
> Was awf'ly sweet and pure
> She interrupted prayers one day
> With a shout of Pig's Manure.[6]

As late as May 21, 1921 Eliot still had not let go of this theme, as we see (with normalized orthography) in a letter to James Joyce.

---

[4]   *Letters*, p. 59.
[5]   *Letters*, p. 86.
[6]   *Letters*, p. 125.

I wish that Miss Beach would bring out a limited edition of
my epic ballad on the life of Christopher Columbus and his
friend King Bolo, but

> Bolo's big black bastard queen
> Was *so* obscene
> She shocked the folk of Golder's Green.[7]

This will do to establish a continuum that culminated in the racy parts
of the original *Waste Land.*   Pound's excision of them is a pity for
three reasons: first, because racy poetry in English is a much
neglected field; more importantly, because Eliot was clearly moving
toward a metamorphosis into a Bad Boy, and Pound arrested this
development, forcing him into the persona of the prim, bespectacled
Thinker, with all his naughtiness bottled up; and finally, because it
erased the connecting passages that made the original *Waste Land*
intelligible.   Let us begin on the title page.

Eliot's original epigraph was not in the Latin and Greek of
Petronius, but in plain English, from *Heart of Darkness.*

> "Did he live his life again in every detail of desire, temptation,
> and surrender during that supreme moment of complete
> knowledge?   He cried in a whisper at some image, at some
> vision, – he cried out twice, a cry that was no more than a
> breath –
> 'The horror!   the horror!'"
> CONRAD[8]

Pound wrote (December 24, 1921), "I doubt if Conrad is weighty
enough to stand the citation."[9]   Eliot replied (January 24[?], 1922),

---

[7] *Letters,* p. 455.
[8] *Facsimile,* p. 3.
[9] *Letters,* p. 497.

"Do you mean not to use Conrad quot. or simply not put Conrad's name to it?   It is much the most appropriate I can find, and somewhat elucidative." [10]   It must have dawned on Eliot, however, that elucidation was not the name of the game, so his letter of March 12, 1922 was extremely unelucidative:

> Cher maitre [*sic*],
> I have substituted for the J. Conrad the following, or something like it:[11]

With the bland finality of a blackjack deal, the present epigraph from *Satyricon* follows, *without* elucidation; Pound had no reply.   Clearly, Eliot was learning that being unelucidative had its advantages.   From now on he addresses Pound as an equal.   It was a victory for Eliot, but also a victory for אומפֿאַרשטענדלעכקייט.[12]

Still, the damage had been done.   Gone, at Pound's behest, was the opening fifty-four line passage of drinking buddies out on the town, *Dubliners* rowdiness that dies down in an almost musical decrescendo to

> So I got out to see the sunrise, and walked home.

I find it a pity that this was left out: it made a very attractive set-up for the present opening line.

There has been a great deal of ink spilled about the Phoenician Sailor, frequently identified with Phlebas.   Yet his importance to the poem is the imagination of subsequent critics, not the poet: Eliot, in the letter of January 24[?] already cited, considered cutting the Phlebas lines out, evidently as non-essential.   The original of this passage

---

[10] *Letters,* p. 505.
[11] *Letters,* p. 506.
[12] This has gone on long enough.   See glossary.

exists in two versions, [13] both representative of the "genteel anti-Semitism" of Eliot's age.   All that remains is

(Those are pearls that were his eyes.   Look!)

The original had "See!"   But more importantly, the original began

> Full fathom five your Bleistein lies
> Under the flatfish and the squids
> Graves' Disease in a dead jew's eyes!
> When the crabs have eat the lids.[14]

Graves' Disease is a form of goiter.   Bleistein would seem to be the same Bleistein as in the 1920 *Burbank with a Baedeker: Bleistein with a Cigar.*

> ...But this or such was Bleistein's way:
> A saggy bending of the knees
> And elbows, with the palms turned out,
> Chicago Semite Viennese.
> A lustreless protrusive eye
> Stares from the protozoic slime...[15]

Here we must pause, and re-orient ourselves; we must not be distracted by our emotional response to writing that would now be considered racy or racist.   I offer the above to illustrate the idea that if Eliot wrote A, and if it was changed to B, that the meaning is lost, and the poem has become a sort of glorified Rohrschach test on the reader's part and a sort of jejune cat-and-mouse game on the part of the poet.   But would Eliot stoop so low as to deliberately insult his readers' good will? Eliot?   Eliot certainly did so in 1924, when the excised "Fresca" lines,

---

[13] *Facsimile,* pp. 119-123.

[14] *Facsimile,* p. 121.

[15] *Facsimile,* p.   131.

somewhat garbled, appeared in *The Criterion* in a contribution by
Vivien Eliot.   Valerie Eliot notes, "It probably amused Eliot to print
'these few poor verses' knowing that only two other people knew their
source."[16]   This is the Royal Nonesuch.

The alert reader may have noticed a loose end: Fresca may be
gone from *The Waste Land,* but she does appear in "Gerontion" (l. 68).
"Gerontion" was intended to be a preface to *The Waste Land;* Pound
cut it,[17] thereby throwing away keys, or at least threads through the
labyrinthine longer poem: the identity of the narrator as an old man;
depraved May; the Jew; the sea.   Similarly, *"Gerontion"* suffers a loss
of clarity with the omission of the characterization of Fresca, who is
now just a name.

Returning to "The Fire Sermon," we note another "Fresca"
episode cut (no great loss); lines 106-115, also cut, explicitly reference
London, a slight loss of vividness; and after the typist's lover

> -- Bestows one final patronizing kiss,
> And gropes his way, finding the stairs unlit...

Pound excises the rest of the quatrain, a considerable loss of vividness,
with the note, "probaly [sic] over the mark."

> And at the corner where the stable is,
> Delays only to urinate, and spit.

Probaly so; but it was Pound who was over the mark with the next
excision.

On the very first reading one is struck by the shortness of IV.
Death by Water.   It is a mere eight lines because Pound cut the first
eighty-three, which is another Dubliners-style "buddy" piece, this one
set on ship, where there is another decrescendo, from jolly cameraderie

---

[16] *Facsimile*, p. 127.
[17] *Letters*, p. 505.

to a storm to the stillness after the storm, that sets up Phlebas.   There
is a striking similarity to the excised first page, that sets up "April is
the cruellest month."   Pound's excisions in both cases have the
dramatic words coming out of the blue, as devoid of context as a
fortune cookie.

The end of *The Waste Land* is Pound's in a very literal sense: it
was he who decided that "The POEM ends with the Shantih, shantih,
shantih."ך

The aesthetic issues raised by examining Eliot's original *Waste
Land* are not hard to understand, but they require fundamental changes
in the way this poem is viewed.   First, the question of authorship: it
will not do to say that the poem is by T.S. Eliot, since Pound's hand is
evident literally from beginning to end.   It is a collaboration.   Next,
the question of unintelligibility: Eliot saw a "reader-friendly"
original progressively obfuscated, and saw the sphinx-like final
product celebrated all over the world.   This sets a pernicious example
for young authors; when I become king I will decree that only Valerie
Eliot's edition be read, so that Eliot's final version can be admired, if it
is the reader's cup of tea, but also so that the reader can see how much
poetry was lost, and (since we now can see that some lines of the poem
were written by Vivien Eliot) exactly what too many cooks did to the
broth.

Although his notoriety came from *The Waste Land,* the poet
would eventually pull back from the brink, unlike Pound, and would
eventually write poetry which would stand scrutiny and repeated
readings, and which would be in his own voice.   And yet there would
be lapses.   I owe Eliot an aesthetic debt for his translation of St.-John
Perse's wonderful poem *Anabasis,* since thirty-odd years ago I did not
know enough French to read the original.   Yet even then I had to
smile at his translation of

l'oiseau chante: "ô vieillesse!...

---

[18] *Letters,* p. 497.

as

the bird sings O Senectus!...

Even then I knew that *vieillesse* was nothing more than the plain, garden-variety French word for "old age;" yet there was Eliot, in midst of a luxuriant poem about barbarian migrations, unable to resist a touch of Latinate stiltedness, since *senectus* is the garden-variety Latin word for "old age."   One could say that, one last time, Ulysses broke free from the mast; but enough classicizing is enough.

Glossary

אומפֿארשטטעענדללעכקייט (um-far-shtend-lekh-keit) is the Yiddish word for "unintelligibility."   I use it as a thought experiment: it does no harm to illustrate absurdity by being absurd.

Modernizing Chaucer's *Anelida and Arcite*

As a rule, background reading is the key to understanding the nuances of Chaucer's poetry. Obscurities of detail and allusion are resolved by investigation of the social and historical influences that the author and his audience took for granted. The exception to this rule is *Anelida and Arcite*. Its theme requires no explanation: a woman's lover leaves her for another. Its action is clear: her grief is described, then she writes a letter to her faithless beau. As far as these aspects of the poem are concerned, the poem could have happened at any time or place.

The difficulties with modernizing *Anelida and Arcite* lie in mirroring the poetic techniques that Chaucer employs, and this leads us inescapably to the last taboo remaining in modern English poetry, the "r-word" – rhyme. Chaucer tells Anelida's story in rhyme royal, a stanza rhyming ABABBCC. After the narrative "set-up," the letter she writes, the complaint, has rhyme schemes that are even tighter: lines 299-307 all rhyme "-ede;" lines 317-332 are AAAB AAAB BBBA BBBBAA, three tetrameters followed by a pentameter. The rhythm is no problem, since English abounds in expressive monosyllables that can fill out a line; the problem is finding a word that has eight rhymes, or in the second case above, two words that have eight rhymes each.

It is no exaggeration to say that the poetic virtuosity of *Anelida and Arcite* is the only facet of the poem that has any interest for us today; this means that rendering this verbal jugglery is the only parameter of a translation that matters. No matter how demanding this may prove to be, the translator must face the parameter of rhyme squarely. It will not do to plead extenuating circumstances, because there are none: there is no conflict between sound and sense in *Anelida and Arcite,* because the sense, as noted above, is too conventional to warrant "bending" the poem for its sake. *Anelida and Arcite* is a rhyming-etude.

Does this require an occasional artificiality or strained rhyme? This question must be answered in two ways, once for the original and once for the translation. Chaucer does not shun words that are rhyme-poor, like *mat* (l. 176), which rhymes with *estat* (l. 178), but not much else. Chaucer's example encourages the translator not to cut corners. On the other hand, the translator is tempted to let things slide at times, because of the fact that occasionally — I wish there were a more graceful way to put this — Chaucer cheats. In the stanza beginning with l. 290 we find lines ending with *unkindenesse, gladnesse, hevynesse* and *witnesse.* In the stanza beginning with l. 204, there is *langwishinge, wepinge* and *compleynynge.* O mighty Caesar, dost thou lie so low? This is a dip into doggerel, as slipshod as rap or the long-forgotten rock 'n' roll outpourings of The Moody Blues. This lapse is made even more glaring by the fact that in the very next stanza Chaucer is at his most brilliant: nine lines with the same rhyme, and moving as effortlessly as prose.

There are two other poetic questions that must be answered: what about half-rhymes and French rhymes? A pause for a terminology check: "moon" and "June" are rhymes; "a maid" and "a mead" (as in Wilfred Owen) are half-rhymes; when Irving Berlin wrote

> *We joined the Navy to see the world,*
> *But what did we see?*
> *We saw the sea.*

he was employing French rhymes, "see" and "sea." Chaucer does not use half-rhymes in *Anelida and Arcite,* so neither do I. French rhymes, however, are another matter. Chaucer and his audience evidently relished them, as with this example from ll. 194-5.

> *Thus serveth he withouten fee or shipe;*
> *She sent him now to londe, now to shippe.*

For all I know, this might have brought down the house at a Chaucer poetry reading. For me, it is simply a groaner.

> *He serves with nary a salary or tip;*
> *She sent him now to land, and now to ship.*
> *Shipe* in Middle English did mean "salary" or "pay." Is my "tip" gratuitous? So be it. I have once allowed "blue" (the color) and "blue" (melancholy), but otherwise, no French rhymes.

A French term, however, is useful: they speak of *le frein vital,* which would literally mean "the vital brake" or "rein." I prefer the rendering "creative restraint." Often, less is more; sometimes, however, anything is too much. The translator must not intrude. My nomination for the absolute worst translation ever involves just this sort of intrusion, Burton Raffel's Englishing of the most famous poem of Indonesia's most famous poet, Chairil Anwar's *"Aku"* ("Me"). Anwar wrote *lari / lari* ("running / running"); Raffel rendered it "running / running / running." *Multum in parvo.* There are several passages where Middle English words correspond exactly to Modern English, as in the stanza beginning with l. 211: we find *hewe* (hue), *trewe* (true), *rewe* (rue) and *newe* (new). Here the temptation is to be clever for the sake of being clever. I decided to let well enough alone, and stuck with the Modern English forms of Chaucer's original.

There were a few vocabulary items that invited retouching. *Hors* (l. 157) does mean "horse," but I translated it as "pet," simply because horses to Chaucer's audience were as common as cats are to us, while to the modern reader the horse is outside his normal range of experience.   Equally distant from our everyday life is *bridil*, in l. 184.

> *His newe lady holdeth him so narowe*
> *Up by the bridil...*

must have resonated with Chaucer's audience, virtually all of whom had controlled a horse this way, perhaps only a few hours before they heard the poet read these lines.   Very few of us moderns have this sort of intimacy with horsemanship, but we have had the experience of controlling the gambols of Man's Best Friend.   Thus,

> *His new love keeps Arcite so tightly reined,*
> *On such a short leash...*

Other exotica were similarly regularized.   Chaucer's *swerd* (l. 212) did not remain a literary-sounding "sword," but became an everyday "knife."   A *tame best* (l. 315) became "a pet."

Some vocabulary changes were "fudging:"   Chaucer's *love* in l. 346 became my "Cupid" for metrical reasons, and his *penaunce* in l. 348 became my "Last Rites" for the sake of vividness.

There was one item I could not find an equivalent for: the song *Chante-pleure*:   try as I might to find an American song whose title would convey "singing-crying," I was unable to do so.   You can't win 'em all.

The reader will have noticed that I end the poem at line 351.   I believe that I have done Chaucer a favor by doing so, for two reasons: first, because the last few lines are spurious, as will be demonstrated by medievalist Jake Lavender in a forthcoming article.   Dr. Lavender's analysis of the manuscript evidence convinced me that the end of Anelide's letter is in fact the end of the poem.   For the sake of completeness, I include an *en face* translation of this non-Chaucer tag as follows.

*   *   *

(The Spurious Ending)

When that Anelida, this woful
quene,
Hath of her hand ywriten in
this wise,
own hand,
With face ded, betwixe pale
and grene,
She fel a-swowe; and sith she
gan to rise,
And unto Mars avoweth
sacrifise
Withinne the temple, with a
sorowful chere,
That shapen was as ye shal
after here.

When Anelida, this unhappy
queen,
Had thus expressed herself
with her

Her face a deadly pale with
touch of green,
She fainted; afterwards, when
she could stand,
355. A sacrifice to Mars the god she
planned
Within the temple, with a
downcast face;
Now listen, and I'll tell what
next took place.

*   *   *

The second reason for explicitly cutting these lines is that critics shy away from uncompleted works, and there are details of *Anelide and Arcite* that still invite critical attention.

The law of supply and demand dictates that there is no future for a modernized *Anelida and Arcite*. On the supply side, the public is drowning in rhyme, from greeting card doggerel to the jump-rope chanting of rap; on the demand side, among modern poetry buffs rhyme is utterly un-hep, un-cool and infra dig. Unless there is a sea-change on both sides, *Anelida and Arcite* will remain as neglected as its leading lady.

*   *   *

Chaucer's *Anelida and Arcite*, lines 155-351

This fals Arcite, sumwhat
moste he feyne,
When he wex fals, to covere
his traitorie,
Ryght as an hors that can both
bite and pleyne,
For he bar her on honde of
trecherie,
And swor he coude her
doublenesse espie,
And al was falsnes that she to
him mente.
Thus swor this thef, and forth
his way he wente.
Alas, what herte myght
enduren hit,
For routhe and wo, her sorwe
for to telle?
Or what man hath the
cunnyng or the wit?
Or what man mighte within
the chambre dwelle,
Yf I to him rehersen sholde
the helle
That suffreth fair Anelida the
quene
For fals Arcite, that dide her al
this tene.

155.   This false Arcite must now
cover his tracks,
Hide his deceit; he irritable
grew,
Just like a pet that purrs, and
then attacks,
Accusing her of the deceits
he'd do,
And swore that she was
two-faced; he saw through
160.   How everything was false that
she would say.
Thus swore the cad, and carried
on this way.
Oh, how could any human
heart endure
Unmoved the recitation of her
woe?
Who'd have the technique to
portray it sure?
Who'd stay to hear, fighting
the urge to go,
166.   Should I recount the hell she'd
undergo,
How queenly Anelida went
insane
For false Arcite, who caused
her all this pain.

She wepith, waileth,
swowneth pitously;
To grounde ded she falleth as
a ston;
Craumpyssheth her lymes
crokedly;
She speketh as her wit were al
agon;
Other colour then asshen hath
she noon;
Non other word speketh she,
moche or lyte,
But "Merci, cruel herte myn,
Arcite!'
And thus endureth til that she
was so mat
That she ne hath foot on
which she may sustene,
But forth languisshing evere
in this estat,
Of which Arcite hath nouther
routhe ne tene.
His herte was elleswhere,
newe and grene,
That on her wo ne deyneth
him not to thinke;
Him rekketh never wher she
flete or synke.
His newe lady holdeth him so
narowe
Up by the bridil, at the staves
ende,
That every word he dredeth as
an arowe;

170.

175.

180.

185.

She weeps and wails; she
sometimes passes out:
She falls down on the floor and
lies stone-cold;
Contorts her limbs as she
tosses about.
She babbles then, with ravings
uncontrolled.
Her face is deathly pale, sad to
behold;
And every word she says is to
entreat,
Just "Mercy, cruel heart of
mine, Arcite."
She keeps on, until she has
reached the point
Where she can't even hold
herself up now,
But helpless lies she, stymied,
out of joint,
None of which gives Arcite the
furrowed brow.
His heart was carefree, nor will
he allow
Himself to fret about his former
flame;
Whether she sinks or swims,
it's all the same.
His new love keeps Arcite so
tightly reined,
On such a short leash, collared,
if you will,
His fear of crossing her keeps
him restrained.

Her daunger made him bothe
bowe and bende,
And as her liste, made him
turne or wende,
For she ne graunted him in her
lyvynge
No grace whi that he hath lust
to singe,
But drof hym forth. Unnethe
liste her knowe
That he was servaunt unto her
ladishippe;
But lest that he were proud,
she held him lowe.
Thus serveth he withoute fee
or shipe;
She sent him now to londe,
now to shippe;
And for she yaf him daunger
al his fille,
Therfor she hadde him at her
owne wille.
Ensample of this, ye thrifty
wymmen alle,
Take her of Anelida and
Arcite,
That for her liste him "dere
herte" calle
And was so meke, therfor he
loved her lyte.
The kynde of mannes herte is
to delyte
In thing that straunge is, also
God me save!

She kept him hopping;
shrewish, she'd instill
Obedience to her caprice, until,

Without her say-so, he'd not do
a thing,
Not make a peep, although
he'd want to sing,
190.   But kept him in his place.
She scarcely cared
That he was servant to Her
Ladyship,
But kept him humble, and she
kept him scared.
He serves with nary a salary or
tip;
She sent him now to land, and
now to ship;
195.   And since she gave him his fill
of her clout,
She had the moony boy turned
inside-out.
Take note of this, all ladies
who are smart,
And learn from Anelida and
Arcite,
That for the joy of calling him
"dear heart"
200.   And was so meek, so he did her
mistreat.
It is the nature of man's heart
to entreat
The one that treats him badly.
Lord above!

For what he may not gete, that wolde he have.
Now turne we to Anelida ageyn,
That pyneth day be day in langwisshinge,
But when she saw that her ne gat no geyn,
Upon a day, ful sorowfully wepinge,
She caste her for to make a compleynynge,
And of her owne hond she gan hit write,
And sente hit to her Theban knyght, Arcite.

The compleynt of Anelida the quene upon fals Arcite.

The one who's out of reach will get his love.
Now we return to Anelida once more,
205. Who gets more listless as the days drag by,
But saw what grief the future had in store.
One day, choked up, with many a tear and sigh,
She thought of giving elegy a try,
And with her own hand she began to write
210. And sent it to Arcite, her Theban knight.

Queen Anelida's Lament on Arcite the Faithless

Proem

So thirleth with the poynt of remembraunce
The swerd of sorowe, ywhet with fals plesaunce,
Myn herte, bare of blis and blak of hewe,
That turned is in quakyng al my daunce,
My surete in awhaped countenaunce,
Sith hit availeth not for to ben trewe;

It stabs me, does this jagged souvenier,
Grief's knife, sharpened by joys that disappear.
My heart, bereft of bliss and black of hue,
Transformed to trembling all my dancing cheer,
215. My confidence to introverted fear.
Since it does no good at all to be true;

For whoso trewest is, hit shal
hir rewe
That serveth love and doth her
observaunce
Alwey til oon, and chaungeth
for no newe.

For whoever's most loyal, most
shall rue
Who serves love and respects
its object dear
Always to one, untempted by
the new.

Strophe

I wot myself as wel as any
wight,
For I loved oon with al myn
herte and myght,
More then myself an hundred
thousand sithe,
And called him myn hertes lif,
my knyght,
And was al his, as fer as hit
was ryght;
And when that he was glad,
then was I blithe,
And his disese was my deth as
swithe;
And he ayein his trouthe hath
me plyght
For evermore, his lady me to
kythe.
Now is he fals, alas, and
causeles,
And of my wo he is so
routheles
That with a word him list not
ones deyne

220. I know myself as well as any
might,
For I loved one who was my
heart's delight,
More than myself, a million
times or more,
And said that he was my
heart's life, my knight,
And was all his, as far as it was
right;
Whenever he was glad, my
heart would soar,
226. When he was moody, death
was at my door;
And he renewed to me his
promise bright
To acknowledge me as his for
ever more.
Now is he false, alas, out of the
blue,
230. And takes no thought of what
I'm going through,
Won't condescend to speak a
word, or deign

To bringe ayen my sorowful
herte in pes,
For he is caught up in another
les.
Ryght as him list, he laugheth
at my peyne,
And I ne can myn herte not
restreyne
For to love him alwey
neveretheles;
And of al this I not to whom
me pleyne.
And shal I pleyne--alas, the
harde stounde!--
Unto my foo that yaf myn
herte a wounde
And yet desireth that myn
harm be more?
Nay, certis, ferther wol I never
founde
Non other helpe, my sores for
to sounde.
My destinee hath shapen hit
so ful yore;
I wil non other medecyne ne
lore;
I wil ben ay ther I was ones
bounde.
That I have seid, be seid for
evermore!
Alas! Wher is become your
gentilesse,
Youre wordes ful of plesaunce
and humblesse,

To soothe, to calm my heart
breaking in two.
For he's been captivated by
some shrew.
Just as he likes, he mocks me
for my pain;

235. Try as I might, I still cannot
restrain
My heart from loving him,
though he's untrue;
Who'll listen to the grief I can't
contain?
And shall I pour my heart out –
woe is me! –
To him who gave my heart this
injury

240. And who still wants my misery
to grow?
No, though I search, there's no
discovery
Of any help to end my agony.

My destiny was fashioned long
ago;
I want none of the lore the
doctors know;

245. I'll stand by what I've spoken
formerly.
What I have said, forever be it
so!
Oh, what's become of your
nobility,
Your soothing words full of
humility,

Youre observaunces in so low manere,
And your awayting and your besynesse
Upon me, that ye calden your maistresse,
Your sovereyne lady in this world here?
Alas! Is ther now nother word ne chere
Ye vouchen sauf upon myn hevynesse?
Alas! Youre love, I bye hit al to dere.
Now, certis, swete, thogh that ye
Thus causeles the cause be
Of my dedly adversyte,
Your manly resoun oghte hit to respite
To slen your frend, and namely me,
That never yet in no degre
Offended yow, as wisly He
That al wot, out of wo my soule quyte!
But for I shewed yow, Arcite,
Al that men wolde to me write,
And was so besy yow to delyte—
Myn honor save--meke, kynde, and fre,

Your kindnesses that were so meekly done,
250.   And your patience and your activity
On my behalf, your mistress, publicly
Proclaimed to be your queen, your only one?
Oh, now I find there's word nor gesture none
You condescend to grant my misery.
255.   Oh, what a price I pay for what I've won!
Now, surely, sweet, although you're he
Who is the cause, unthinkingly
Of the frustration killing me,
Your manly reason should make you forego
260.   Hurting your friend, me, fatally,
Who never in the least degree
Offended you, as wisely He
Who knows all things, may rid my soul of woe!
But since, Arcite, I let you see
265.   My letters, unreservedly,

And did you every courtesy --

Meek, kind, and free as honor'd let me go,

Therfor ye put on me this wite,
And of me rekke not a myte,
Thogh that the swerd of sorwe byte
My woful herte through your cruelte.
My swete foo, why do ye so, for shame?
And thenke ye that furthered be your name
To love a newe, and ben untrewe? Nay!
And putte yow in sclaunder now and blame,
And do to me adversite and grame,
That love yow most--God, wel thou wost--alway?
Yet come ayein, and yet be pleyn som day,
And than shal this, that now is mys, be game,
And al foryive, while that I lyve may.

270.

275.

280.

You pay me back with calumny,
Take me for granted brazenly,
You cut me with your cruelty,
The knife of grief you wield to hurt me so.
My darling foe, why do you thus, for shame?
Do you think that this will increase your fame
To find a new conquest, and make me crawl?
To be the object of slander and blame,
To be hostile to me, and ruin the name
Of her who – God knows! – loves you most of all?
But if you change your mind, and someday call,
We'll put this all behind us, like a game,
And I'll forgive, whatever may befall.

Antistrophe

Lo, herte myn, al this is for to seyne
As whether shal I preve or elles pleyne?
Which is the wey to doon yow to be trewe?

Lo, heart of mine, all this is just to say,
Will I only lament, or make headway?
To make you faithful, just what must I do?

For either mot I have yow in
my cheyne
Or with the deth ye mote
departe us tweyne;
Ther ben non other mene
weyes newe.
For God so wisly upon my
soule rewe,
As verrayly ye sleen me with
the peyne;
That may ye se unfeyned of
myn hewe.
For thus ferforth have I my
deth [y-]soght?
Myself I mordre with my
privy thoght;
For sorowe and routhe of your
unkyndenesse
I wepe, I wake, I faste; al
helpeth noght;
I weyve joye that is to speke
of oght,
I voyde companye, I fle
gladnesse.
Who may avaunte her beter of
hevynesse
Then I? And to this plyte have
ye me broght,
Withoute gilt--me nedeth no
witnesse.
And shal I preye, and weyve
womanhede?—
Nay! Rather deth then do so
foul a dede! --

I lock you up and throw the key
away,
285. Or you must sunder us with
death some day;:
There is no other choice, only
these two.
God pity my soul for what it's
been through,
As pitiless you watch my life
decay;
That in the end you'll see my
colors true.
290. Is this the reason why I have
death sought?
I'm killing myself with my
secret thought.
Grieving and bitter at your
heartlessness,
I weep, can't sleep, can't eat,
and all for naught;
I can't keep up with small talk
as I ought,
295. I shun all visitors in my
distress.
Who better knows how loving
can depress
Than I?   To this extreme I
have been brought,
All innocent – but am here,
nonetheless.
Shall I forget my self-respect,
and plead?
300. No!   Rather death than do so
foul a deed!

And axe merci, gilteles--what nede?

And yf I pleyne what lyf that I lede,
Yow rekketh not; that knowe I, out of drede;
And if that I to yow myne othes bede
For myn excuse, a skorn shal be my mede.
Your chere floureth, but it wol not sede;
Ful longe agoon I oghte have taken hede.
For thogh I hadde yow to-morowe ageyn,
I myghte as wel holde Aperill fro reyn
As holde yow, to make yow be stidfast.
Almyghty God, of trouthe sovereyn,
Wher is the trouthe of man?
Who hath hit slayn?
Who that hem loveth, she shal hem fynde as fast
As in a tempest is a roten mast.
Is that a tame best that is ay feyn
To fleen away when he is lest agast?

And ask forgiveness? For what wrong?
What need?
And if I complain of the life I lead,
You don't hear a single word, I concede.
No litany of vows made could I read
305. To excuse me; you'd despise me, guaranteed.
Your blooming looks will never produce seed.
Oh, long ago I ought to have taken heed.
Because, if you came back tomorrow, I
Might just as well hope to keep April dry
310. As hold on to you and make you steadfast.
Almighty God, in whom there is no lie,
Where's man's fidelity? How did it die?
Whoever loves him, finds his love won't last,
As when a tempest snaps a rotten mast.
315. Is a pet really tame who'll always try
To run, and when startled can't be held fast?

Now merci, swete, yf I mysseye!
Have I seyd oght amys, I preye?
I noot; my wit is al aweye.
I fare as doth the song of Chaunte-pleure
For now I pleyne, and now I pleye;
I am so mased that I deye;
Arcite hath born awey the keye
Of al my world, and my good aventure.
For in this world nis creature

Wakynge in more discomfiture
Then I, ne more sorowe endure.
And yf I slepe a furlong wey or tweye,
Then thynketh me that your figure
Before me stont, clad in asure,

To profren eft and newe assure
For to be trewe, and merci me to preye.
The longe nyght this wonder sight I drye,
And on the day for thilke afray I dye,
And of al this ryght noght, iwis, ye reche.

320.

325.

330.

335.

Now, dear, don't be too hard on me!
Have I spoken offensively?

I'm not myself, as you can see.
I'm doing as romantic torch-songs do:
I'm low, then high as I can be,

Then seem to die, confusedly;
Arcite has carried off the key
Of my whole world, and dreams that won't come true.
No creature – search the whole world through –

Spends its day more depressed and blue
Than I, nor lives with keener rue.
And if I nap for two minutes or three,
It seems that you come into view,
Standing before me, dressed in blue,

To promise all will be like new,
For my forgiveness, your humility.
The long night through, this sight's before my eye,
During the day, this anguish makes me die,
But you see nothing of this; there's the catch!

Ne nevere mo myn yen two be drie,
And to your routhe, and to your trouthe, I crie.
But welawey! To fer be they to feche;
Thus holdeth me my destinee a wreche.
But me to rede out of this drede, or guye,
Ne may my wit, so weyk is hit, not streche.

These eyes of mine will nevermore be dry,
Appealing to your better self, I cry.
Alas!   It is too far away to fetch;
Thus destiny keeps me a helpless wretch.
340. To extricate myself, no guide have I:
My wit, weak as it is, that far can't stretch.

Conclusion.

Then ende I thus, sith I may do no more.
I yeve hit up for now and evermore,
For I shal never eft putten in balaunce
My sekernes, ne lerne of love the lore.
But as the swan, I have herd seyd ful yore,
Ayeins his deth shal singen his penaunce,
So singe I here my destinee or chaunce,
How that Arcite Anelida so sore
Hath thirled with the poynt of remembraunce.

I finish here, since I can do no more.
I give it up for now and evermore,
345. For never shall I risk my peace of mind,
Nor try my luck at learning Cupid's lore.
But like the swan, as I have heard before,
Shall sing the Last Rites, to his death resigned,
I sing the fate that came from Fortune blind,
350. How that Arcite has stabbed me to the core,
And left this jagged souvenier behind.

Saroyan in Taiwan

In May of 2005, when I was considering relocating to Taiwan, I had a most instructive job interview at what I will call "University A." It was a meandering interview, and I had a growing feeling that the committee and I were not on the same page. Finally, one of the interviewers, clearly showing impatience, asked me rather sharply, "What part of English do you want to teach?" Bewildered, I stammered out "Accent reduction, I guess." The interviewers began to roll their eyes and shake their heads. The question was put to me again, even more sharply, in a multiple-choice format: speaking, comprehension, reading or writing? When it became evident that I was still bewildered, the committee members evidently decided that either I was playing dumb or that I really was dumb. The interview meandered to an end a few minutes later.

I did not get the job.

In the academic year of 2005-6, after I had relocated to Taiwan, I had a most instructive part-time job at what I will call "University B," where I taught one section of writing and one of conversation. In the latter, I was amazed at how the students reacted with incredulity, then annoyance, then resentment, to my insistence that they distinguish between "plan" and "plane" and "Sam" and "same." It was a conversation class, they protested, not a pronunciation class. They had come to converse, and they had conversed, and that was that. The students in the writing class reacted with incredulity (although without annoyance or resentment) when I asked them to "tweak" their compositions, that is, polish them, tighten them up, fine-tune their message. They pointed out, accurately, that their compositions were no worse than those in their textbook.   I in turn pointed out that that the compositional models in their textbook were written by other EFL students.

(It was a required textbook, let me add, and the first that I had ever seen based on the theoretical model of the blind leading the blind.)

These composition students, however, saw nothing wrong with the blind leading the blind.   They had come to write, and they had written, and in a few minutes it would be time for lunch, and that was that.

I did not keep the job.

In September of 2005, immediately after settling in at my present job at Chinese Culture University, in Taipei (which I will not call "University C"), I had my first encounter with the sort of materials commonly used in language labs in Taiwan.

I know a few things about language labs.   From March of 1971 to April of 1972 I practically lived in one, at the Defense Language Institute in Monterey, California, USA.   I was enrolled in the 47-week course in Indonesian, which met five days a week, six hours a day during that year.   I learned firsthand the value of transcription exercises as an aid not only to listening comprehension, but also to writing style, since there is no better way to familiarize oneself with a language model than by listening and re-listening until one can write out every blessed word.   My experience, then, taught me that the real result of language lab work was not auditory competence (this was only a short-range benefit), but a sense of literary style, provided that the model was a worthy one.

Thirty years later, in Taiwan, I found myself looking through language lab materials that either ignored or contradicted everything I knew to be true.   I immediately informed my boss, Language Center Director Prof. Terry Wu, that I would not use them, and gave reasons.

In case today's audience contains any of my interviewers from "University A," who view English teaching as inherently fragmented, before dealing with the writing fragment, I will deal with another fragment or two, hopefully in a form that they will find suitably fragmentary.   For the rest of us, note that in the following passage, the word "auditory" or "listening" is interchangeable with "writing" or "composition."

One does not use visual means to teach auditory skills, and it was the amount of effort lavished on the visual elements of these course materials that was striking: the design and layout were not just colorful, they were garish; the photographs and drawn illustrations were not just plentiful, they were superabundant, not to mention arresting, even provocative.   This is the Hollywood Gospel: visual appeal sells.   Listening comprehension, however, is not visual. Speaking is not visual.   Those who do not understand this may try either one on the telephone.   Stressing visual appeal undercuts the message of the importance of competence in auditory skills.

To be fair, there was an audio component, but its content was thin, predigested, predictable: trite, adolescent chit-chat in a preposterous "Global Village" class, where Michiko, Miguel, Mohammed and Marie-France are talking gravely about courtship customs in Patagonia. Had I seen this material six months earlier, I would have shrugged it off as merely more of the same bad textbook writing that I had seen since the '70's, when I started in EFL.   In the context of Taiwan, however, it was the missing piece of the puzzle.

Why were my conversation students at "University B" so smug? They were not smug; they had in fact triumphed over their material, but they had been shielded from knowing just how thin, predigested and conventional that material was.   As to why the conversation class was bewildered by what they saw as my mixing of skills, the answer was to be found in the attitudes of the teachers at "University A," which saw English as a fragmented discipline.

Practice does not make perfect.   Practice makes one the same, or, as my students at "University B" probably say to this day, the Sam.   It is perfect practice that makes perfect; more exactly, it is perfect practice of the opposite skill: to improve one's pronunciation, one listens.   To improve one's writing, one reads.

Why were the writing students satisfied with their mediocre writing? Because they had mediocre models to follow.

Prof. Wu gave me permission to revive a dictation program I had developed during my years at the Language and Culture Center of the University of Houston: it had no visual elements at all, and it presented English as a unified discipline. The work to be transcribed was William Saroyan's novella *The Human Comedy*.

At the University of Houston, I had prefaced the *Human Comedy* project with a "warm-up" exercise involving a commercially available recording of Malcom X's speech "Ballots or Bullets," with a list of words and cultural notes that students were not expected to know, and the results were satisfactory: it was a good warm-up for dictation of real-life English. With that in mind, the first year at the CCU Language Center I prefaced the *Human Comedy* dictation with commercially-available recordings of two episodes from the American radio serial *Gunsmoke* ("Land Deal" and "The Photographer"), but dropped this warm-up thereafter. The students did well with the recordings as dictation exercises, but because of the compression inherent in the radio drama genre, I was spending much of the class time (and break time, too) answering the students' questions about content and culture. They could transcribe the exclamation of the "Chester" character when he said "Well, forevermore," but were fascinated by the fact that the way he said it sounded like "Wail, fur ever mower," and their curiosity was piqued by the phrase itself. It was good to explain a few characteristics of Southern U.S. pronunciation, and Southern speakers' tendency toward euphemism, but the explanations took time away from the students' work, which was dictation. At present the assigned dictation is *The Human Comedy* and only *The Human Comedy*.

This novella was published in 1943. It concerns the lives of a family in an idyllic small town. The central character, a fourteen-year-old boy, has an after-school job as a telegraph messenger, and the variety of messages he has to deliver moves the story forward.

I have made this overview of *The Human Comedy* intentionally bare-bones, because it is easy to get bogged down in the circumstances surrounding it. Its author was colorful, there is a Hollywood element in its inception and transmission, it contains allusions to the classics and Americana that might tempt the teacher to get off-track. Those who are interested in the story behind the story are welcome to wander off in search of it; in literature, however, the answer to the question, "Who wrote this?" is "Who cares?" What counts is what is on the page, and the reader is best left undistracted by the persona of the author, even on those occasions when the popular perception of the author happens to be true.

What is important for the EFL class is the novella's excellence and its clarity. Saroyan dedicated it to his mother, whose native language was Armenian. "I have written it as simply as possible, with the blending of the severe and the light-hearted which is especially yours, and our family's," Saroyan writes in the preface.

As to the lab methodology, the students bring blank cassette tapes to the lab's technical man, Mr. Sun, who makes copies from a master recording, read by me previously. Each student has a tape player on which he can play and replay the recording as many times as it takes for him to understand it and write it down. The teacher walks around the lab with the book, looking over the students' work as he walks, and choosing this or that student at random for detailed correction. For an example of the results in practice, let us imagine that the dictation is the opening of *The Human Comedy*'s first chapter.

The little boy named Ulysses Macauley one day stood over the new gopher hole in the backyard of his house on Santa Clara Avenue in Ithaca, California. The gopher of this hole pushed up fresh, moist dirt and peeked out at the boy, who was certainly a stranger, but perhaps not an enemy.

We learn from our mistakes, and these two sentences provide a variety of mistakes for the student to make; one could almost say, invite the student to make.   First, however, it must be understood that most of the sentence is easy: a Chinese EFL student at the college level should have no difficulty understanding and correctly transcribing the first four words, although the minor error "name" for "named" sometimes occurs.   By contrast, there is no reason why a Chinese EFL student should know the low-frequency name "Ulysses," nor is it a disgrace not to know which orthographic variant of the family name Macauley the author prefers.   This is one kind of mistake: the brick wall.   It is important that the student not be shielded from indecipherable content: frustration is good, and in any case help is not far away.   The student does the best he can; once the correction is made, he is expected to remember it, but there is the underlying message that it is no disgrace not to know a word that one cannot possibly know.   "Africa" for "Ithaca" is an understandable mistake, given the similarity in sound between the words, as is "golfer" for "gopher," and the student's choice of a plausible word is nothing to be ashamed of; although it is still an error, it is a "soft" error.   "Picked out" for "peeked out," however, has the diagnostic function of showing that the student needs work differentiating the vowels in comprehension, and, it may be inferred, in speech.   The same is true for "suddenly" instead of "certainly," or "hall" for "hole."   "Whole" for "hole" reveals a different kind of confusion.

It is important to recognize, however, that at the same time that the student is performing an auditory task, he is also performing a literary one: he is examining a fine piece of writing, one that can serve as a model for his own creative efforts.   The purpose of studying literature is to improve one's English.   Saroyan's straightforward style is a model not only for writing, but also for speech, and is diagnostic for pronunciation.   The student is introduced to a work that is of recognized excellence, one that is also understandable and duplicable by lower-level EFL college students in Taiwan.   The presentation of the work is gradual, beginning as a dictation exercise, and proceeding to the student's critique of the novella's style, characterization and plot.   (Usually this begins abruptly, in the form of a student's exclamation, "This is not a comedy! How can he call this a comedy?") The student learns that with discipline and economy of means, good writing is not a distant goal, but a standard of work that applies even at the lower levels of English competence.

So much for what *The Human Comedy* is. It is important, however, to recognize that much of the novella's worth is found in what it is not. Put another way, it is not trendy.

A Chinese student learns about his past via the "Three-Character Essay," an elegant and concisely-written historical summary.

> When he looks at the West, however, he is presented with impossible contradictions: journals full of scientific marvels, but also hip-hop videos full of overpaid, gyrating nitwits; a vast complex of educational institutions, but one which produces detailed descriptions of the Emperor's new clothes; an economic system of efficiency and opportunity, but a Hollywood culture that glorifies plastic surgery and dope. There is no way that the Chinese student can separate the wheat from the chaff by himself, and the odds are not much better if his teacher or other western contact is a dreamy, out-of-focus New Ager.[1]

This is not merely an abstraction of the Culture Wars. The practical problem in the EFL classroom is that, unless this cultural ambivalence is removed, it becomes a pedagogical stumbling-block. As a thought experiment, let us turn the tables: let us imagine a class where the students are dreamy, out-of-focus New Agers who are asked to prepare a speech on why global warming is a hoax. Imagine their anguish, their resistance to this assignment! Imagine how much good will it would cost the teacher, whether he realized it or not! As another thought experiment, let us turn the tables back where they should be,

---

[1] Skupin and Wu 216.

and ask if the textbooks currently in use have gratuitous cultural baggage that clashes with the student's life-experience.   If the answer to this thought-question is "yes," then *The Human Comedy* should be on the teacher's list of possible textbooks.

Being free from cultural ephemera is good, but it is also important that the reading be informative about topics that are permanent. English is rooted in the facts of life in the Anglosphere.   Otherwise, it is pidgin.   There is plenty of overlap between the attitudes and activities inside the Anglosphere and those outside it, and *The Human Comedy* is full of observations about these permanently valid subjects.

Ahab Astray

My first encounter with *Moby-Dick* was a typically American one: I saw the movie first. It was 1956; I was seven years old; the film excited my imagination, but only in the way that Disney's *20,000 Leagues Under the Sea* did, since in arid west Texas "ocean" and "whale" were concepts as abstract as algebra; in the end, though, the excitement passed: it was just another movie. In my twenties I discovered that Melville's novel is not just another book, and a quarter-century of avid re-readings intervened before I saw the old film – video, now – and saw it with new eyes.

From the standpoint of criticism, this 1956 cinematic adaptation is a very interesting time capsule, or, if you will, a sampler of the critical opinions of that era. I found that its most striking feature was the portrayal of Ahab. In Hollywood the medium is the message, and casting Gregory Peck as the Pequod's captain made for a glamorous, broad-chested, debonair Ahab that did not square with the way I understood the character at all.

Background reading on the subject, however, revealed that interpreting Ahab as a hero was very typical of critical analysis in that era.

> Ahab's drive is to prove, not to discover... He seeks to dominate nature, to impose and to inflict his will on the outside world... This is Ahab's quest – and Ahab's magnificence. For in this speech Ahab expresses more

forcibly than Ishmael ever could, something of the impenitent anger against the universe that all of us can feel.[1]

"All of us" evidently includes the writer, literary critic Alfred Kazin. These are strange words coming from a cultivated man of letters: after all, being likened to Captain Ahab is not exactly a feather in one's cap, any more than being likened to Captain Bligh would be. Yet Kazin is unequivocal: for him the important thing about Ahab is his refusal to go gentle into that good night.

> To the degree that we feel this futility in the face of a blind impersonal nature that 'heeds us not', and storm madly, like Ahab, against the dread that there's 'naught beyond' -- to this extent all men may recognize Ahab's bitterness, his unrelentingness, his inability to rest in that uncertainty which, Freud has told us, modern man must learn to endure. Ahab figures in a symbolic fable; he is acting out thoughts which we all share. But Ahab, even more, is a hero; we cannot insist enough on that.[2]

A hero. We may take it, then, that Kazin would have had no problem with Gregory Peck as Ahab. Before moving to the question of whether or not Herman Melville would have had a problem with Gregory Peck as Ahab, we must note that Kazin is just getting warmed up.

> And because Ahab, as Melville intended him to, represents the aristocracy of intellect in our democracy, because he seeks to transcend the limitations that good conventional men like Starbuck, philistine materialists like Stubb, and unthinking fools like Flask want to impose on everybody else, Ahab

---

[1]   Beaver 338
[2]   Beaver 339-40

speaks for the humanity that belongs to man's imaginative vision of himself.[3]

It would seem that Kazin might have preferred that the role of Ahab had been played by John Wayne, or Charlton Heston, or perhaps even by Ike.

I found Kazin's petulance incomprehensible: would he have considered Helen Keller a failure for not raging against the dying of the light? Sirhan Sirhan identified the woes of the Palestinian people with Robert Fitzgerald Kennedy; did that make him a visionary? Doubtless some rent-a-prof could coax Transcendentalism from between the lines of *Mein Kampf*, but must we believe everything with footnotes?

Ahab's case is simple: if the word "insane" means anything, then Ahab is insane. If I regard the evil in the world as incarnate in a certain goldfish, then I am insane; if I identify the evil in the world with this or that trout, or with "Flipper," then I am insane; and so up the maritime ladder. *Moby-Dick* is about insanity, the contagiousness of insanity, and how one copes when authority gets skewed.

But back to the critics: Kazin's views were in no way extreme in the fifties. An even more grandiose vision of Ahab from that decade is to be found in Henry A. Murray's "In Nomine Diaboli," read at the first centennial celebration in 1951. Murray offers two hypotheses.

> The first of them is this; Captain Ahab is an embodiment of that fallen angel or demi-god... Captain Ahab-Lucifer is also related to a sun-god, like Christ, but in reverse.[4]

Before moving to the second of Murray's two hypotheses, a digression is called for, to show just how seriously, how pedantically,

---

[3] Beaver 339
[4] Hillway 40

Murray takes the words "in reverse."   On the subject of Fedallah he writes:

> The Arabic name "Fedallah" suggests "dev(il) Allah," that is, the Mohammedans' god as he appeared in the mind's eye of a Crusader.[5]

The uninitiated may complain that equating "fed-" and "dev-" is not criticism, but dyslexia; but this is rather like complaining about left-handedness among baseball pitchers.   Boustrophedon argumentation of this kind abounds in literary criticism, and is traditionally accepted without demur.   Nor is it valid to waggishly counter-propose "feed-Allah" or "fad-Allah" or even "fuddle-Allah," since the author was writing ex cathedra.   Murray was a university professor of clinical psychology, whose life changed in

> 1925, when, as he says, the reading of *Moby-Dick* "catapulted him out of the field of biochemistry into the landless sea of the unconscious mental processes."[6]

For the record, the reader should note that the version of Murray's "In Nomine Diaboli" included in Harold Bloom's anthology is quite watered-down: in the 1951 original perorations in praise of psychology's big names abound.   With this in mind, the author's second hypothesis, that a psychologist should look at *Moby-Dick* in psychological terms, is an anticlimax.

> Stated in psychological concepts, Ahab is captain of the culturally repressed dispositions of human nature, that part of personality which psychoanalysts have called the "Id."[7]

---

[5]   Hillway 40-41
[6]   Hillway Bloom 132-33 Bloom 134 Bloom 138 Bloom142 Bloom 134
[7]   Hillway 42

Be that as it may, Murray is not the only voyager on "the landless sea of the unconscious mental processes." P. Adams Sitney focuses on the Ahab matter in much the same spirit when he discusses the question in "The Symphony" (Melville's Chapter CXXXII), "Is Ahab, Ahab?"[8] Sitney asks follow-up questions: Is Ahab, Ahab who provoked the Lord God of Israel?[9] Is Ahab Ishmael?[10] Is Ahab Fedallah?[11] Although this rhetorical question is answered by the Captain himself two chapters later ("Ahab is for ever Ahab, man."), Sitney proposes answers for each of these questions in terms that echo Murray's analysis in tone, even though his essay was written thirty years later. Besides proving the durability of the glamorous-Ahab hypothesis, however, Sitney includes a very instructive error:

> In a useful note Willard Thorp pointed out that Peleg means "division"; Captain Peleg divides the lays of the ship's income.[12]

Ignoring the jots and tittles of the matter, and ignoring the fact that Sitney has not even glanced at the absolutely vital question of whether or not Herman Melville himself had been notified of this etymology, we see that this line of reasoning instantly collapses under its own weight when extended to Ahab. Does the root פלג (PaLaG, PeLeG as a noun) mean "divide?" It can; but it is also true that the root אהב ('aHaB) means "love," as can be verified by looking in any Hebrew reference work. Captain Love? An Ahab played by Brad Pitt? No: Ahab is for ever Ahab, and the only place he can be found is in *Moby-Dick*; and the only place elucidation can be found besides that novel is in antecedents known to Herman Melville.

---

[8]   Bloom 132-33
[9]   Bloom 134
[10]   Bloom 138
[11]   Bloom 142
[12]   Bloom 134

Limiting ourselves to the novel, and taking the long view, what do we have?   A man engages to perform a service, but instead indulges in a caprice.

Let us imagine that we board a plane in Houston bound for Boston; shortly after take-off the pilot announces that he is flying us to San Francisco instead, and harangues us passengers to the effect that, although we might have thought that we wanted to go to Boston, we really should have wanted to go to San Francisco, and in any case, going to San Francisco is the most important thing in the world to him. Is he being heroic?   In a movie, would he be played by Gregory Peck?

Although the messianic-Ahab school of thought had a long life, it eventually began to get some competition.   A case for Ahab's insanity was made in 1976 by Henry Nash Smith, who was explicit not only in his general opinion, but even in specifics:

> We have... two stages in the development of Ahab's madness: a first stage, of indeterminate length, in which his exasperations accumulate and burst forth in the fury of his futile single-handed attack on the whale; and a second stage, following the mutilation, during which Ahab becomes insane. But because his madness is a "cunning and feline" monomania, he is able to conceal "the mad secret of his unabated rage" while he plans the "audacious, immitigable, and supernatural revenge" that is the hidden goal of the voyage of the Pequod.[13]

This analysis leads us directly to Melville's fund of experiences, specifically to his father-in-law, Judge Lemuel Shaw.   This jurist presided over a number of cases involving insanity; McCarthy cites one especially, the 1844 case of one Abner Rogers, a prison inmate who had been prompted by inner voices to kill a warden.   Judge Shaw's charge to the jury is worth noting, because it will foreshadow the testimony of my star witness in the matter of Ahab's madness.

---

[13]   Hayes 187

The character of the mental disease relied upon to excuse the accused in this case, is partial insanity, consisting of melancholy, accompanied by delusion. The conduct may be in many respects regular, the mind acute, and the conduct apparently governed by the rules of propriety, and at the same time there may be insane delusion by which the mind is perverted... [T]he act was the result of the disease, and not of a mind capable of choosing: in short that it was the result of uncontrollable impulse, and not of a person acted upon by motives, and governed by the will.[14]

Ahab's mind is certainly acute: Jeff Todd analyzes the stagecraft of "The Quarterdeck" for its rabble-rousing potential, and finds that Ahab's "pitch" to the crew is a finely-honed ritual that appeals irresistibly to the men's weaknesses. Although Todd never answers his preliminary question, "Why does the austere, Quaker-bred Ahab continually rely upon such extravagant display?"[15] his exposition of the techniques of Ahab's demagoguery concludes that the captain is realistic, even shrewd in his manipulation.

In 1993 Julian Markels presented a literary study titled *Melville and the Politics of Identity*, but whose subtitle was much more accurate: *From King Lear to Moby-Dick*. Markels' discussion of the correspondences between Ahab/Pip and Lear/Fool are especially persuasive,[16] but he points out fainter (though still discernable) echoes of *Macbeth*,[17] *Othello*[18] and *Hamlet*.[19] The case is clear for Shakespeare's unhinged leading men being antecedents that influenced Melville. Unhinged antecedents for an unhinged Ahab seemed right to me, but even I had to draw the line with Adamson's 1997 *Melville,*

---

[14] McCarthy 53
[15] Todd 4
[16] Markels 62
[17] Markels 65
[18] Markels 64
[19] Markels 62

Shame, and the Evil Eye: A Psychoanalytic Reading.   Here the pendulum had swung too far: everyone is mad, according to Adamson.   I insist that a square reading of the text identifies Ahab as the madman; he maddens his crew, but only in a figurative sense.   To keep the literal and figurative separate in these overused terms, I avail myself of Seamus Heaney's title for his 1983 translation of the medieval Irish classic *Buile Suibne Geilt* ("The Tale of Mad Sweeney"):   he called it *Sweeney Astray*; I refer to Ahab Astray.

My star witness for an Ahab Astray is not a modern critic of this or that school, but Herman Melville himself.   Let the reader recall the charge of Judge Shaw cited earlier, and then consider Melville's opinion as expressed on pages 353-54 of the Penguin *Billy Budd*.

> But the thing which in eminent instances signalizes so exceptional a nature is this: Though the man's even temper and discreet bearing would seem to intimate a mind peculiarly subject to the law of reason, not the less in heart he would seem to riot in complete exemption from that law, having apparently little to do with reason further than to employ it as an ambidexter implement for effecting the irrational.   That is to say: Toward the accomplishment of an aim which in wantonness of atrocity would seem to partake of the insane, he will direct a cool judgment [sic] sagacious and sound.   These men are madmen, and of the most dangerous sort, for their lunacy is not continuous, but occasional, evoked by some special object; it is protectively secretive, which is as much as to say it is self-contained, so that when, moreover, most active it is to the average mind not distinguishable from sanity, and for the reason above suggested: that whatever its aims may be – and the aim is never declared – the method and the outward proceeding are always perfectly rational.

These men are madmen.   Ahab Astray is one of them.

Sixteen Hamlets

Of all the participants in the semester-long special course at Chinese Culture University that we called The *Hamlet* Project, I am the luckiest. Prof. Timothy Fox must be credited with the inspiration for the project and the labor of setting it up; Prof. Kid Lam managed the project once it was underway, with great energy and tact; Prof. Lucy Yao lent her prestige and credibility to our dealings with our guest scholars and with the CCU bureaucracy; the guest scholars themselves went to great lengths to present learned and thought-provoking lectures; and the students had a lot of hard reading and challenging ideas to deal with, and not a lot of time to absorb it all.

I just showed up, and was lucky enough to be in the right place at the right time. This means that my knowledge of the project is actually quite narrow: I can only speak about what I saw, the end result of all the preparatory work that made The *Hamlet* Project possible.

What I saw most of was the students, so I will begin with them. On paper there were ten of them, although that is not quite the whole story. Three other students showed up, but I refused to seat them; based on their previous performance (they were former students of mine), I concluded that they were not up to the task.

A mystery soon developed as to the students who were not ejected: there were ten on the class roll, but only nine would show up. We had, then, the opposite of the Biblical "Where are the nine?" We knew where the nine were, but where was the tenth? Eventually she appeared – to take the final exam, evidently with the assumption that she could receive a passing grade in the course without attending the course.   She was mistaken.

There were, then, really nine students, but again that is not the whole story.   It is better to say that there were *only* nine students.   I consider myself very fortunate to be teaching at Chinese Culture University, and hope to continue teaching here for years to come.   My only complaint, and that since my first day on the job, is about the size of classes here, so it was a luxury to have a class that was not a human sea.   The intimacy of the setting was a stimulant for the students, since they could not hide in the herd, and had to be ready to be put on the spot for recitation at any moment.

These students were most instructive as to a pedagogical problem that had vexed me since I arrived in Taiwan back in 2005:   I refer to the Jekyll-and-Hyde nature of the Taiwanese student.   The Taiwanese student is exceptional for his intelligence, creativity and powers of observation – except in class.   In class, the Taiwanese student exhibits what can only be called trance behavior, giving the impression of being unintelligent, uncreative and unobservant to an almost theatrical degree.   After class, say, when the students come by during my office hours, they are again intelligent, creative and observant.   An incident occurred during the visit of Prof. C. H. Perng of National Taiwan University that I found fascinating: Dr. Perng's subject was the complicated matter of the monologues in *Hamlet*, and he was in fine form that day, posing provocative questions with his customary extroverted delivery; break time; "Any questions?" he asked; silence; "All right, then, let's take a break."   Suddenly the students' hands were in the air, and they were full of questions.   The announcement of a break was like the starting gun of a race, in which the students were suddenly intelligent, creative and observant again.   However, instead of describing the event as the announcement of the beginning of a break, I believe it would be more fruitful to describe it as the end of a class period.

My previous experience with what I have called trance behavior had come from two sources: first, the years I spent teaching with the

Refugee Program at Houston Community College in Houston, Texas, USA in the 1980's. There my students were mostly from Vietnam, Laos and Cambodia, and most were suffering from some degree of what is now called post-traumatic stress disorder. The other source was the six months I spent travelling and teaching in Colombia in the 1970's, where even then the violence that had plagued that country for so long had already resulted in profound post-traumatic stress disorder that was widespread enough to be considered a national characteristic.

Neither of these experiences, however, had prepared me for dealing with the mercurial personality of the Taiwanese student. The incident with Dr. Perng, though, gave me a clue: the on-again, off-again trance behavior of my students was the result of specific triggers, whose source I identified, by process of elimination, as originating in the trauma, albeit "lite" trauma, of the Taiwanese classroom. The account of my subsequent identification and elimination of specific triggers will be for a separate paper, at another conference, but the gradual changes in my classroom style and the students' response, will be observable on the video recording of the classes made by Prof. Lam and posted on the class website.

The video recording leads me to what it recorded, the content of the course. This can be summed up as either studying *Hamlet* or studying about *Hamlet*. Most of our class time was devoted to the former, nothing more complicated than a close reading of the play. I determined that it would be better to understand part of the play thoroughly than to skim over the whole thing, the scenario I have elsewhere described as "where the teacher pretends to teach, and the students pretend to learn." We read meticulously, beginning at the beginning and "digging" through Act II, scene 1. If it seems that in reading only one act of *Hamlet* the students did no more than scratch the surface of this great work, so be it; I have been scratching the surface of Hamlet for over forty years.

In addition to this close reading, I touched on the matter of studying about Hamlet, introducing the sources (the First Folio, the Quartos, and the strange German play called *Der bestrafte Brudermord* ["the punished fratricide"], which is clearly a garbled version of a Quarto *Hamlet*).   I mentioned Shakespeare on the Restoration stage in the context of theatrical conventions, and the Olivier *Hamlet* in the context of the influence of critical commentary on performance.   The majority of the critical commentary was presented by the guest speakers, although their topics prompted further close readings of passages beyond Act II, scene 1.   Before Prof. Perng came, he requested that the class be familiar with the end of Act III, scene 3, where Claudius attempts to pray and is discovered by Hamlet. Accordingly, we did a close reading of that passage to prepare for the Prof. Perng's very stimulating ideas.   Prof. So of Wenzao Ursuline College of Languages asked that the class be familiar with the "All the world's a stage" speech in *As You Like It* (Act 2, scene 7), but the students had already read that one in the Shakespeare survey class in the previous semester.   Prof. Beatrice Lei, also of National Taiwan University, requested that the class have a good overall knowledge of the plot of *Hamlet* prior to her talk, and I was only too happy to comply, after having seen the students' answers on a diagnostic test written by Prof. Fox and administered earlier in the semester.   The students were rather hazy on fundamental questions like "Who is Polonius?" so it was worth a detour of an hour or two to get us all on the same page.   Like young students everywhere, they at first showed every indication of waiting until the last minute to get really serious about the course, but the enthusiasm of our guest speakers was contagious, and the students "caught fire" sooner and to a greater degree than I had hoped.

I caught fire, too.   Every time I read *Hamlet* or see *Hamlet* performed I find something new, yes, even after forty years of it, so in addition to opening new horizons for the students, the Project's guest speakers brought fresh insights to me.

More important than their individual commentary was the fact of their diversity of outlook, their different approaches to *Hamlet*.   The students were clearly intrigued by this variety.   Prof. So had a bookish perspective that reflected his wide reading, while Profs. Perng and Lei had a performance emphasis: Dr. Perng provided a nuanced mini-performance of the Hamlet/Claudius scene referred to earlier, in which he played the king on his knees, while one of the students, lurking behind him and about to "stab" him with a blue dry-board marker, was the prince.   Dr. Lei presented an outward-looking survey of Chinese-opera versions of *Hamlet* that have been staged in recent years, as well as a remarkable series of observations on the female characters in the tragedy.

Our last speaker, Prof. Timothy Fox, now of National Ilan University, presented a wide-ranging and technologically sophisticated survey of pseudo-*Hamlets,* from the very fine play *Rosencrantz and Guildenstern are Dead* through opera and ballet adaptations down, or perhaps I should say down, down, down to the latest of the tiresome travesties that have followed *Hamlet* through the centuries.

We end where we began, with Dr. Fox, the originator of the project and its last guest speaker.   Since the three most important things in education in Taiwan are tests, tests and tests, I should mention that there was, according to the terms of the Ministry of Education grant, a final exam, and a final project where the students made videos of various scenes, but I will not dwell on them.   They were made insignificant by the breadth and depth of the material studied.   A big subject like *Hamlet* takes a long time to internalize, so a "snap" exam at the end of the course is as pedagogically useless as digging up a tree the day after it is planted to see if its roots are growing.   If these students and I should cross paths in five or ten years, it will be interesting to see what they have done with the excellent introduction to *Hamlet* that Profs. Fox, Lam, Yao, So, Perng, Lei and your humble servant have provided to the nine students who began their exploration of *Hamlet* this year.

The Language Landscape

in Israel at the Turn of the Eras

This essay will address questions related to the sociolinguistics of the Middle East about the time of Christ. What languages were spoken in the Middle East generally? Did rabbis speak Greek? Were they bilingual in Aramaic and Greek?

Our starting point will be Jerusalem. Beginning at a center and moving outward is a sensible way to organize our material; Jerusalem has the additional advantage of being the center toward which things moved.

> In the time of Herod and the Roman prefects or procurators up to the Jewish war Jerusalem was not only the capital of Jewish Palestine but was at the same time a metropolis of international, world-wide significance, a great 'attraction' in the literal sense, the centre of the whole inhabited world. Nor was it the 'navel' only for pious Jews of the Diaspora but also an interesting place for educated Greeks, pagans and adventurers.[1]

This will facilitate the enumeration of the many sociopolitical currents of the day, currents relative to our topic because they were linguistically "tagged," as will be seen. Another fact that is convenient to our study is the importance of the man at the center of the center, Herod, who had become king in 37 B.C., and whose

---

[1] Hengel 11

dynamic reign had to a decisive degree set up the linguistic status quo in which Jesus lived.

The four main strands of this status quo in Jerusalem were Latin, Greek, Hebrew and Aramaic.

The status of Latin is easily summarized.

> Of the four languages mentioned above, Latin was the least common and was restricted largely to Roman soldiers and Imperial officials. As a result, it was used only in certain places in the city at certain times, for example, in the Antonia fortress on pilgrimage festivals when large contingents of soldiers were brought in to keep order, or in the procurator's residence when he visited the city.[2]

Latin was the language of political and military rule; Greek was the language of an invasion of a different kind. Krauss, of whom more later, would begin the preface of his great dictionary by saying, *Alexanders Schwert and Aristoteles' Geist haben den Orient auf Jahrhunderte hinaus für griechische Sprache und Cultur erobert.* ("Alexander's sword and Aristotle's spirit conquered the East for Greek language and culture for centuries on end.")   In fact, Hellenistic culture challenged Jewish tradition on many other fronts besides philosophy and the military: it also manifested itself in architecture, theatrical performances, gymnastics, chariot-races, hunting, music, and Homer. It was a slick, seductive, pervasive "package deal" that was in direct competition with the simple godliness of earlier times. Long before Herod came to power, Jewish rulers had begun to identify themselves on coins as "philhelene," [3]although, as we shall see, Herod's passion for Greco-Roman culture went much deeper, and had a more profound influence. Besides the

---

[2]   Levine 73
[3]   Hegel 8

intangibles, there were hard political and economic realities that Herod's policies brought about.

> Money flowed into the city from the didrachma tax, which Herod had had safely transferred to Jerusalem thanks to the pax Romana, and a good deal more money came into the city through the sacrifices of the festival pilgrims.[4]

The didrachma was a half-shekel contribution to the temple, previously collected and stored locally.   This unprecedented concentration of hard cash stimulated the city's economy, which in turn financed grandiose building projects in the Hellenistic style, which in turn fostered what we would now call tourism.   Jerusalem had become a boomtown.

> The temple with its bank was one of the richest in antiquity, and time and again tempted Roman generals and officials to lay hands on its treasure.   The Jewish population reacted to this sacrilege with disturbances.[5]

The word "tourism" above was used advisedly; in addition to Jewish pilgrims, there were Gentile visitors who came to admire the city.

> So Jerusalem was without doubt one of the most impressive and famous temple cities in the Roman empire, and even for pagans was surrounded with an almost 'mystical' aura.[6]

Times were flush.

---

[4]   Hengel 12
[5]   Hengel 12
[6]   Hengel 13

The daily life of at least the upper classes fully matched the standard of luxury and comfort to which people in the Roman empire were accustomed.[7]

Levine gives three reasons for these enormous changes.[8]   First and foremost was the pax Romana, which facilitated travel, trade and communication. As a result, Jerusalem became linked more firmly than ever to a network of urban centers in the Roman East.

A second factor was Herod's status as a client king.   It was imperative that he keep his kingdom integrated as much as possible into the Roman world.   By his great agility and sagacity he was able to maintain and strengthen political connections time and again in the course of his career.   It must not be thought, however, that Herod was simply making Jerusalem a Potemkin village to impress the Romans. True, his building projects included not only a theater and a hippodrome, but also that quintessentially Roman institution, an amphitheater for gladiatorial combats,[9] and he earmarked funds to make sure that they were run in style.

> Herod constructed these buildings with the intention of introducing typical Roman institutions in his capital, thus placing Jerusalem in the cultural forefront along with other major urban centers of the East.   However, Herod was not content with simply erecting these structures; he also allocated considerable sums of money to promote quadrennial spectacles to which he invited the foremost athletes and performers of the time.[10]

Herod's Greco-Roman sympathies were genuine.   Nicolaus of Damascus, Herod's close advisor and teacher, takes note of his

---

[7] Hengel 12
[8] Levine 45ff
[9] Levine 55
[10] Levine 56

enthusiasm for Greek philosophy, rhetoric, and history.[11] His personal commitment in this regard was reinforced by the people of his court, many of whom were non-Jewish, but all of whom bore either Greek or Latin names, a clear indication of their cultural proclivities.

A third factor that had considerable influence on the language milieu of Herodian Jerusalem was the dramatically expanding Jewish Diaspora, whose centers were characterized by their extensive geographic distribution and by their social and political integration into the surrounding societies in terms of language, names, official titles, and institutional forms.

Herod encouraged links between his court and these distant communities not only by correspondence, but also by permanent relocation.

> There was a constant and lively interchange with all the centres of the Diaspora. Thus Herod first brought the priest Ananel from Babylonia and later the priest Simon, son of Boethus, from Alexandria to Jerusalem.[12]

Herod's motives may have been other than purely ecumenical: by bringing in outsiders, he was edging out Jerusalem's "old guard" with individuals loyal to him.

> Moreover, Herod's rebuilding of the Jerusalem Temple on a monumental scale served not only as a source of inspiration for Jews everywhere but also as an inducement and attraction for many to visit the city, often in the pilgrimage festivals. The multitudes streaming to the city in the course of the year were in no small degree composed of Jews from far-flung Diaspora communities. Thus, representing a microcosm of the entire Roman world, the pilgrims who gathered in

---

[11] Levine 48
[12] Hengel 14

Jerusalem brought within its walls a wide range of cultures that could help balance any inclination toward isolation that may have existed among some native Jerusalemites.[13]

Acts 2:9-11 gives a very impressive breakdown of the origins of these pilgrims; concentrating for the moment on Greek speakers, we find that there were synagogues that catered to them.   Acts 6:9 mentions some of these "diaspora synagogues,"

> in first place that of the Λιβερτινοι, i.e. the Jewish freemen from Rome.
> In these Greek-speaking synagogue communities in Jerusalem the Septuagint was used...[14]

Greek, then, was not only the language of a resident Hellenizing elite, but was a language that regularly received "reinforcements" from abroad.

> While it is difficult to assess what percentage of the population spoke Greek or even understood it, the use of Greek in Jerusalem apppears to have been far more widespread than either Latin or Hebrew.   That some rabbis sought to ban the teaching Greek in the early second century C.E. while others facilitated a Greek translation of the Bible by Aquilas further indicates the widespread use of the language.[15]

The mention of rabbis recalls the two questions at the beginning of this paper: Did rabbis speak Greek?   Were they bilingual in Aramaic and Greek?   At least one was: Flavius Josephus was able

---

[13] Levine 54
[14] Hengel 13
[15] Levine 80

> to translate those books into the Greek tongue, which I
> formerly composed in the language of our own country...[16]

Although it could be argued that the latter language was Hebrew, I take his statement to mean Aramaic, since he later speaks of sending this earlier version to the Jewish communities "in the north," which would have been in the regions where Aramaic was the lingua franca. Nothing by Josephus is extant except for his Greek works, so the matter must rest there.

As to rabbis in general, they knew a great deal of Greek without studying it, and Latin, too, because of the extensive use of loan words from those languages in rabbinical literature. Samuel Krauss's two-volume *Griechische und Lateinische Lehnwörter im Talmud, Midrasch und Targum* goes on for hundreds of very dense pages, and Sperber's dictionary of these loan-words, although nowhere near as massive, is still quite extensive.

Beyond the presence of these foreign words in the literature, there is evidence that the rabbis consciously set out to become multilingual. Some of their "homework" is still extant.

> A ubiquitous feature of scholarship in the ancient world was
> the creation of lists — a penchant rather wittily dubbed
> Listenswissenschaft — and among such lists in early Rabbinic
> literature we find linguistic features regularly itemized —
> concordances of the use of words or phrases, statistics of the
> frequency of words in the Hebrew Bible, and so forth.[17]

Enumerations of words and passages to be memorized also include bilinguals: Hebrew-to-Aramaic, Hebrew-to-Greek, and Greek-to-

---

[16] Josephus 427

[17] Alexander 77

Latin lists exist, and in various formats: verse-against-verse, phrase-against-phrase, word-against-word.[18]

There can be little question that the most ubiquitous language of first-century Jerusalem was Aramaic. Levine gives several types of evidence that he considers decisive in according Aramaic primacy among the languages used in the city. The first was the use of Aramaic translations of the Scriptures in this period — in synagogue settings, at the very least.

> This custom is well known from rabbinic literature of the second century C.E., but it probably existed beforehand as well...The fact that [such] translations existed and played a central role in the synagogue liturgy of the time indicates the degree to which the populace at large did not understand Hebrew and thus required an Aramaic translation.[19]

Levine also cites literary and numismatic evidence, and quotes several "to whom it may concern" letters addressed to the Jewish community at large, whose language is Aramaic.[20]

Hebrew, the fourth strand of the language status quo, was a language that was doomed:

> After the Bar-Kokheba revolt (132-135 C.E.), the population of Judaea was decimated, and the rabbis and their disciples moved to Galilee, bringing with them the... literature written in Middle Hebrew. Here they quickly became assimilated to the Aramaic-speaking environment, and in one to two generations spoken Middle Hebrew became extinct (perhaps

---

[18] Alexander 87ff
[19] Levine 82
[20] Levine 83

with the exception of dispersed and culturally rather unimportant settlements in Judaea).[21]

During the life of Jesus, however, Hebrew was still widely spoken, although it was a language on the decline, if not on the defensive. Those in power "tagged" themselves with Latin; those who were debonair and fashionable "tagged" themselves with Greek; Hebrew became the "tag" for nostalgia: the good old days, the ancient virtues, nationalist as opposed to cosmopolitan.

Since Jerusalem was the center of this cosmopolitan culture, it would follow that Hebrew would be of marginal importance there.

> Other than funerary inscriptions, we have little evidence for the use of this language among the population in general.[22]

It would also follow that the opposite would be true in the more traditional parts of the country.

> The most telling evidence for the widespread use of Hebrew in Jewish circles of the first century comes from outside Jerusalem.   The written material found in the Judaean Desert, relating to both Qumran and Bar Kokhba, attests to the use of Hebrew not only as a literary language but also, in the   case of the latter, as a living tongue used in letters and documents. However, the relevance of this data to the question of languages spoken in Jerusalem is unclear.[23]

It must remain unclear because of Hebrew's role as a religious language.   Catch-phrases may be employed by a speaker with no real competence in a language of prestige, the way a modern American

---

[21] Paper 4

[22] Levine 74

[23] Levine 75

with no Latin may refer to "an ad hoc committee."   Hebrew exists in first-century Jerusalem in funerary inscriptions; Latin exists in modern America in funerary inscriptions, but in neither case can that be taken as evidence for vernacular use.   Relevant to our subject,

> Let us look at Qumran.   Scriptural texts, canonical and apocryphal, have been found there in Hebrew, Aramaic, and Greek.   Was the community, then, trilingual?   Or was what we stumbled upon at Qumran a kind of geniza where exemplars of the Septuagint, for instance, were identified as Scripture and so preserved as an act of reverence and piety, even though no one could read what was written there?[24]

Whether anyone in the cloisters of Qumran could read them or not does not change the fact that each language had its role in Israel at that time: Greek and Aramaic were cosmopolitan, Hebrew was home-grown.   Since the cosmopolitan elements dominated urban society, however, Hebrew was also the language of the powerless, the aggrieved, and of those who dreamed of setting things right.   This identification had begun at least two centuries before the life of Christ, and

> had obvious theological and political overtones since it was first raised by Ben Sira and then, in a more violent and radical form, by the Maccabees.[25]

The radicalness would not stop with the Maccabees, however, as the Dead Sea Scrolls would reveal.   This literature was radical in two senses.   First, it was "retro."   Its very calendar was Davidic in inspiration.

---

[24] Paper 162
[25] Paper 159

> The new evidence would seem to indicate that the Qumran community, whose self-appellation was the "Sons of Zadok," was divided into subgroups bearing the names of David's priestly courses.[26]

Second, it was militant. Messianic literature was not unique to the Judaean wilderness; it is a topic in the writings of the contemporary Alexandrian philosopher Philo.[27] Philo also writes approvingly of ascetic Jewish sects in Egypt.[28] What distinguishes the Qumran community is the fierceness of its nationalism and the otherworldliness of its utopianism.

> It is for these reasons that we felt it more appropriate to refer to the movement we have before us as the 'Messianic' one, and its literature as the literature of 'the Messianic Movement' in Palestine... In fact, what one seems to have reflected in this Qumran literature is a Messianic élite retreating or 'separating' into the wilderness... The militancy of this spirit will be unfamiliar to many readers — although those with a knowledge of militant Puritanism of seventeenth-century England — particularly under Cromwell — and thereafter in America will recognize it. It is a militancy that is still very much part of the Islamic spirituality as well. It is this kind of spirit which shines through the texts as we have them...[29]

This militancy would lead to disaster, the extiction of Hebrew and the survival of Latin, Greek and Aramaic. It is an irony of history that the twenty-first century would find these latter "big three" on the wane, and Hebrew reborn as the national language of modern Israel.

---

[26] Wacholder xi
[27] Collins 134ff
[28] Feldman 522ff
[29] Eisenman 11-12

Bestride the Narrow World:

John Fiske as a Model for Cather's "Professor"

An analysis of the main character in *The Professor's House* must take into account the seamlessness of Willa Cather's transformation of the personality of Godfrey St. Peter. The other characters influence him subtly, his memories exert a gentle but constant psychological pull, and he mellows as the book closes; *The Professor's House* does not lend itself to pinpoint analysis of this or that incident as a turning point.

Cather's starting point, however, is another matter. After the publication of *The Professor's House* she wrote of the relevance of what classical musicians call sonata form: "But the experiment which interested me was something a little more vague, and was very much akin to the arrangement followed in sonatas in which the academic sonata form was handled somewhat freely."[1] I trust that the reader will indulge a further touch of musical jargon: in a sonata, before the development (the variations on the melodies) and recapitulation (the final repetition of the melodies), there must be an exposition (the playing of the melodies in their simple form). A similar concept applies to a theme and variations: it begins with a straightforward statement of the melody to be varied. We cannot focus on any moment in the elusive modulations the professor's character undergoes, but there is nothing elusive about his personality at the beginning of the story.

---

[1] Giannone 153

"Why, man, he doth bestride the narrow world / Like a colossus!" exclaims Shakespeare's Cassius, commenting on the title role in *Julius Caesar* (1.2.135).   The narrow world of Willa Cather's *The Professor's House* is similarly dominated by the character of Godfrey St. Peter in the early chapters, not only because he is the focus of the novel, but because of the way he lords it over the other characters. He bullies them, charms them, out-talks them, eludes them.   Although various critics have identified source material that accounts for the physical appearance of St. Peter and to the characteristics of his scholarship, there has been no persuasive identification of antecedents that might have inspired his overbearing personality.   This essay will argue that Cather's model was John Fiske, an icon from the generation previous to Cather's, a man whose reputation as a popularizer of science was comparable to that of the late Carl Sagan in our day.

First, however, let us take a closer look at this overbearing personality.   I choose the lengthy monologue in Chapter 5 of Book I[2] to approach the question.   It is safe to infer that this passage is significant, because it is the first, and by far the longest statement of his opinions that the professor makes, almost two full pages.   We do not hear the question that St. Peter is responding to, but it evidently involved the role of science in human affairs.   I call the reader's attention to the following excerpts, which I italicize.

> "[Science] has given us a lot of ingenious toys; they take our attention away from the real problems, of course, and since the problems are insoluble, I suppose we ought to be grateful for distraction."[3]

On the face of it, Cather seems to commit two literary sins here: first, she proposes ideas that clash with her readers' life experience.   *The Professor's House* was published in 1925, when their memories of the

---

2   Cather 54
3   Cather 54

scientifically-enhanced horrors of World War I were still fresh.   Did the author expect them to consider chlorine gas an ingenious toy? Gas masks a distraction?   What was she thinking?   Second, she undercuts the characterization that she has spent fifty-three pages establishing, that of a serious, respected academician.   Folderol is acceptable in the mouths of major characters only when there is irony or deception, as when Hamlet is stringing Polonius along.   Is the professor stringing his students along?   Is Cather stringing her readers along?   There is nothing to suggest that this is so.   There is no disclaimer or distancing the professor from these ideas in the subsequent conversation he has with his wife and son-in-law, who have overheard the monologue; on the contrary, his wife speaks of St. Peter's soliloquy as pearls before the swine: "I wish he wouldn't talk to those fat-faced boys as if they were intelligent beings.   You cheapen yourself, Godfrey.   It makes me a little ashamed."[4]   The reader is left, then, with the conclusion that the professor's folderol must be taken at face value, and with a sense of puzzlement as to why Hamlet has started talking like the grave digger.

> "Science hasn't given us any new amazements, except of the superficial kind we get from witnessing dexterity and sleight-of-hand."[5]

More folderol: by 1925 the airplane had given innumerable new amazements to all who had eyes to see.   In the arts, 1925 was the year of the premieres of Chaplin's *The Gold Rush*, Keaton's *The General*, and Valentino's *The Sheik*.   Take away the science and these masterpieces would be just long-forgotten dumbshows.   Take away the science and Cather's readers would never have heard Caruso, and on and on.

---

[4]   Cather 56-7
[5]   Cather 55

> "It's the laboratory, not the Lamb of God, that taketh away the sins of the world."[6]
> I will not comment on this sally here, but will have occasion to recall it later.
> "Art and religion (they are the same thing, in the end, of course) have given man the only happiness he has ever had." [7]

Lake Michigan is neither an art nor a religion.   Cather writes that having to leave Lake Michigan at age eight made St. Peter unhappy,[8] and that he relocated to Hamilton College because of its proximity to Lake Michigan.   Cather repeatedly portrays the professor as happy when he is swimming in Lake Michigan.   How do we square this with St. Peter's airy assertion that man's only happiness comes from some sort of clumping of art and religion?   Lake Michigan is neither an art nor a religion.   Nor are sunsets, wildflowers or birdsong.

> "But I think the hour is up.   You might tell me next week, Miller, what you think science has done for us, besides making us very comfortable."[9]

The reader wise in the ways of academia may think that next week it might be wise for Miller to keep his mouth shut.

Several candidates have been proposed as real-life models for Cather's Professor; since at least two of them are persuasive, it may be inferred that St. Peter is a composite.   That Cather utilized prototypes frequently is certainly no secret.   In an early interview, speaking about her method, she said, "'Imagination,' which is a quality writers must have, does not mean the ability to weave pretty stories out of nothing.   In the right sense, imagination is a response to what is

---

[6]   Cather 55
[7]   Cather 55
[8]   Cather 21
[9]   Cather 56

going on – a sensitiveness to which outside things appeal.   It is a composition of sympathy and observation.'"[10]

Before considering the characteristics that make John Fiske a likely prototype, let us summarize the state of the question vis-à-vis the figures whose candidacy already seems likely.   We begin with a vade mecum, John Marsh's *A Reader's Companion to the Fiction of Willa Cather*, under the entry "St. Peter, Napoleon Godfrey," and we find our first nominee, a professor named Esquerré.   "He [St. Peter] has some of Willa Cather's own tastes, prejudices, and passions, but physically, he resembles Dr. Edmond Esquerré whom Cather knew when she lived in Pittsburgh."   In *Pittsburgh Portraits* [11] Elizabeth Moorhead Vermorcken described Dr. Esquerré very much as Cather describes St. Peter.   "The Esquerrés...were good friends of [socialite and friend of Cather's] Isabell McClung..."[12]

There is nothing against this idea, as far as it goes; but it is, after all, only an impression, a thumbnail sketch.   L. Brent Bohlke is much more persuasive in the case he makes, the remarkable number of similarities between St. Peter and the French painter Delacroix in his "Godfrey St. Peter and Eugène Delacroix: A Portrait of the Artist in *The Professor's House?*"   Ferdinand Victor Eugène Delacroix was born on 26 April 1798, near Paris.   After a classical education at the Lycèe Impèrial and the deaths of both his parents he entered the École des Beaux-Arts.   Cather must have become acquainted with the art of Delacroix from her visits to Paris, since his murals and frescoes decorate many public buildings and his paintings are scattered throughout the Louvre and other places.[13]   She refers to the artist in *The Professor's House* when St. Peter regrets

---

[10] Bohlke 35
[11] Vermorcken 86-101
[12] Marsh 658
[13] Bohlke 36

that he had never got that vacation in Paris with Tom
Outland...to stand with him before the monument to Delacroix
and watch the sun gleam on the bronze figures...[14]

Delacroix's appearance was one of the most striking things about him.
The poet Gautier described him thus:

> His pale olive complexion, his thick dark hair which remained
> so to the end of his life, his fierce eyes with their feline
> expression, shielded by long lashes whose points curved back,
> his subtle, thin, slightly wrinkled lips over the magnificent
> teeth and under the shadow of a slight moustache, his
> powerful chin with its robust width emphasizing its
> stubbornness, these composed a face possessed of a wild
> strange, exotic, almost disquieting beauty.

His friend Baudelaire wrote of the energy and the impatience that
emanated from him:

> His eyes which were large and black...seemed to drink in and
> absorb and savor the light, his glossy and abundant hair, his
> expression of cruelty from the constant straining of the will –
> in a word, his whole person seemed to suggest an exotic origin.
> Many a time while watching him, has it occurred to me to hark
> back in dreams to the ancient sovereigns of Mexico, to
> Montezuma.

Bohlke comments, "It almost seems as if we have met that man before
somewhere."[15]   He goes on to cite Cather's description of the
professor:

---

[14] Cather 236
[15] Bohlke 23

[Godfrey St. Peter] had a long brown face, with an oval chin over which he wore a close trimmed Van Dyke, like a tuft of shiny black fur. With his silky, very black hair, he had a tawny skin with gold lights in it, a hawk nose, and hawk-like eyes – brown and gold and green. They were set in ample cavities, with plenty of room to move about, under thick, curly, black eyebrows that turned up sharply at the outer ends, like military moustaches.

His wicked-looking eyebrows made his students call him Mephistopheles–[16]

The artist, too, was accused of being Satanic, and on one occasion his rival, Ingres, had gone about opening the windows in the Louvre after Delacroix had departed, "exclaiming that he left behind him a smell of sulphur."[17]

Other details from the artist's Journal will remind the reader of *The Professor's House.* "A thousand difficulties in installing ourselves in lodgings. We think the thing horrible and unbearable, and we end up by getting used to it...The repairing of my stove made me take a walk to the museum"[18]

The faulty stove is not the end of the similarities between the French painter and Cather's main character. Both come from nonreligious households, yet both work when church services are going on. Delacroix wrote: "I used to like particularly to work on Sundays in the churches; the music of the services quite exalted me..." Their work is often regulated by the ringing of the church bells because of their proximity to them.[19] The Angelus bells are mentioned in *The Professor's House*; Delacroix died just after the morning Angelus had rung.[20]

---

[16] Cather 4-5
[17] Bohlke 23
[18] Bohlke 25
[19] Bohlke 31
[20] Bohlke 22

Having mentioned the artist's death (in 1863), it is worth mentioning parenthetically that his Journal was published in 1893-95 (in three volumes), and so would have been available to Cather.

Cather also specifies a similarity in musical tastes.

> Another affinity between the artist and the Professor is their taste in music. On Christmas Day, when St. Peter returns from his study and prepares for the holiday dinner, "his wife heard him humming his favorite air from Matrimonio Segreto while he was dressing..." This comic opera, by Cimarosa, was performed often in Paris during Delacroix's lifetime. He tells of having seen it performed on at least three different occasions and calls it "perfection itself..."[21]

Equally convincing is the case presented by Patricia Lee Yongue in "Search and Research: Willa Cather in Quest of History," for archaeologist Adolph Bandelier being a prototype of St. Peter the academician.

> Willa Cather's Professor is by no means Bandelier in all or even several major respects, but he certainly seems to cut Bandelier's figure insofar as his scholarly aims and approaches to history are concerned.[22]

Similarities between Bandelier and St. Peter include archival work in Spain, writing on "Fray Marcos" [of Nizza],[23] and interest in the American Southwest.[24]   Just as with Delacroix, however, the parallels are limited to the aesthetic requirements of the novel.

---

[21] Bohlke 33
[22] Yongue 34
[23] Yongue 35
[24] Yongue 36

> Even in her probable drawing upon the life and writings of
> Bandelier, Willa Cather made the characteristic literary
> decisions concerning what she would and would not use, and
> what she would modify to suit her nature and that of Professor
> St. Peter.[25]

We may take it that this would be true as well in the case of other
candidates; and the question is still open, since Godfrey St. Peter's
personality has parameters that square neither with Delacroix nor with
Bandelier.

John Fiske is mentioned by name in *The Professor's House,*[26] but
I know of only one Cather specialist, Dr. Yongue, who has suggested
that this allusion might be meaningful.   I was a student of Dr. Yongue;
she knew of my musical background, and called my attention to an
essay by Fiske, his review of the American premiere of the oratorio "St.
Peter," by John Knowles Paine, later included in Fiske's *The Unseen
World,* published in 1876.   Yongue suspected that there was
important material there, but had been put off by Fiske's turgid musical
jargon.   The question of whether Willa Cather made use of this essay
must be preceded by two preliminary questions: first, what does this
essay mean, taken at face value?   Second, how much could Willa
Cather have understood?

The first question could just as easily be paraphrased: What
does Fiske's mumbo-jumbo boil down to?   For mumbo-jumbo it is,
an exact musical analogue to what Thorstein Veblen would later
achieve in economics: trivia expressed as ponderously as possible.
I cite the following passages as examples of theoretical bombast.   The
printed page is not the medium for translation into musical terms, so I
ask the reader to take on trust my assertion that the musical reality
behind the rhetoric is quite prosaic, even trite: it can be demonstrated

---

[25] Yongue 37
[26] Cather 22

on a guitar; on a ukelele.   I cannot improve on the Chinese expression:
Big thunder, small rain.

> ...the dominant chord of C major asserts itself, being repeated,
> with sundry inversions , through a dozen bars, and descending
> through the interval of a diminished seventh.[27]
> ...the entrance of the trombones upon the inverted
> subdominant triad of C-sharp minor, and their pause upon the
> dominant of the same key.[28]
> The cadence prepared by the 6/4 chord... seems to be
> especially disliked by Mr. Paine, as it occurs but once or twice
> in the course of the work.   In the great choruses the cadence
> is usually reached either by a pedal on the tonic... or by a
> pedal on the dominant culminating in a chord of the major
> ninth, as in the final chorus; or there is a plagal cadence, as in
> the first chorus of the second part; or if the 6/4 chord is
> introduced...its ordinary effect is covered and obscured by the
> movement of the divided sopranos.[29]

Here I must protest that even by Fiske's obfuscatory standards,
"plagal" is gratuitous.   A plagal cadence is nothing more than an
"amen" cadence.   There is a satisfying poetic justice, therefore,
when Fiske runs out of "gas," as when instead of the standard term
"Picardy third," he flails around with a clumsy circumlocution.

> Something of the same feeling, too, attaches to those cadences
> in which an unexpected major third usurps the place of the
> minor which the ear was expecting.[30]

---

[27] Fiske 1876, 349
[28] Fiske 1876, 350
[29] Fiske 1876, 356
[30] Fiske 1876, 357

In a word, from a musician's point of view, Fiske's "St. Peter" article is folderol.

We pass to the second question, that of Cather's understanding of what Fiske wrote. I suspect that Willa Cather did not understand very much. Consider her reference to sonata form cited earlier: *The Professor's House* is not in sonata form at all. Sonata form is an integrated tripartite melding of two melodies: usually musicians describe it in the terms I have written of above: exposition, where the themes are presented, the development, where the themes alternate in varied form, and the recapitulation, where the themes are repeated in a form similar to their first appearance. *The Professor's House* is tripartite (Professor-Tom Outland-Professor), but its parts are distinct, not integrated. A musician would refer to this pattern as ABA, the form not of a sonata, but of a minuet. This is not the only example of Cather's overreaching herself. In *One of Ours* she writes that the last waltz at a dance was *Home Sweet Home*, which is not a waltz at all: a waltz is in triple time, whereas Stephen Foster's song is duple. In the same novel, a ruined violin was "a Stradivarius," which is not likely: every Strad in the world has been catalogued, and frequently named, so Cather would seem to have uncritically adopted a cliché. I infer from these little inaccuracies that Cather would not have been able to verify the prosaic musical reality behind Fiske's pretentious terminology by going to the piano, or by picking up a ukelele.

Appleton's Cyclopædia of American Biography has an entry on the life of John Fiske. It is important because it was published in 1894, and so was therefore a part of the cultural background of Cather's era. It is also important because John Fiske himself probably wrote it; Fiske was co-editor of this volume, and so presumably had some input on what was said about him. We infer, therefore, that this is "p.r.," Fiske the way Fiske wanted himself presented. There is not one word about music in this sketch; the stress is on the academic positions he had held, and on his fame as a Bad Boy of the *cause célèbre* of the day, Darwinolatry.

At an early age inquiries into the nature of human progress led him to a careful study of the doctrine of evolution, and it was as an expounder of this doctrine that he first became known to the public. [31]

We note from his letters, however, Fiske proposed a sort of "soft" evolution. Writing to his mother on March 31, 1872, he informs her that

On Friday noon I gave my concluding lecture in Boston – on the "Critical Attitude of Philosophy Toward Christianity", in which, as the consummation of my long course, I throw a blaze of new light upon the complete harmony between Christianity and the deepest scientific philosophy. It was received with immense applause, you ought to have been there.[32]

The letter also is worth citing for its intense subjectivity.

I suppose there was some eloquence as well as logic in it, for many of the ladies in the audience were moved to tears... Several people told me that their lives would be brighter ever after hearing these lectures; that they had never known any pleasure like it; and as these things were said with moistened eyes, I have no doubt they came from the heart.[33]

Just how interested in evolution is Prof. Fiske? How interested is he in objective facts, as opposed to playing to the gallery? In *The Discovery of America*[34] he discusses the "possible origin of adobe

---

[31] Wilson 469
[32] E. Fiske 211
[33] E. Fiske 211
[34] Fiske 1892, 85

architecture" in a learnèd way, but we note a persistent staginess, the poseur's constant striving to be clever, even extending to his footnotes.

> With the woman rests the security of the marriage ties; and it must be said, in her high honour, that she rarely abuses the privilege; that is, never sends her husband 'to the home of his fathers' unless he richly deserves it. But should not Mr. Cushing have said "home of his mothers," or perhaps, "his sisters and his cousins and his aunts?" For a moment afterward he tells us, "To her belong all the children; and descent, including inheritance, is on her side."[35]

There is something depressing about this sort of jauntiness: showing off one's erudition is one thing, but showing off one's knowledge of Gilbert & Sullivan is a little sad. For an equally flat essay in comedic hubris, the reader may recall St. Peter's quibble about the laboratory and the Lamb of God.

John Knowles Paine, the composer of "St. Peter," left a memoir of Fiske's musical attainments, but a prefatory note about him is in order: Paine was a Maine man who studied in Germany. Although the grand style he learned there is no longer in fashion, his shorter works are still in the active repertory of choruses, and especially of church choirs, all across the United States. Paine reports that

> [Fiske] was not allowed to take music lessons in his boyhood, yet in spite of this, he taught himself to play the piano and to sing. Certainly it was a remarkable proof of his genuine talent, that he was able to acquire sufficient skill to play from memory certain sonatas of Beethoven, nocturnes of Chopin, and piano pieces of Schubert, etc. He played with true expression and conception. He also gained a knowledge of

---

[35] Fiske 1892, 89

> Harmony and Counterpoint by reading text-books...In brief, music was his great passion.[36]

Well and good: and how did Paine know all this?

> On the 6th of September, 1864, at 11.30 a.m., John Fiske and Abby Morgan Brooks were married ... at Appleton Chapel, Harvard University, Cambridge.   This was the first wedding in Appleton Chapel, and Professor Paine played the organ on the occasion. [37]

Well and good: Paine and Fiske were old friends when "Paine's 'St. Peter'" was written; but there is not a word of this possible conflict of interest in Fiske's essay.   Is this not high-handed?   Hypocritical? Autocratic?   A lot like Prof. St. Peter?

We have answered our question: what Cather got from Fiske's essay, besides the name "St. Peter," is the tone of his discourse, the bumptiousness, the superciliousness that is the professor's trademark in the early chapters of *The Professor's House*.   Comparison of any paragraph in "Paine's 'St. Peter'" with the Professor's speech where he puts young Miller down, will show a correspondence of tone that is uncanny.   This is what Cather absorbed, and what she reproduced in *The Professor's House*.

---

[36] Clarke 84
[37] Clarke 299

Hyperion to a Satyr:

The Strange Case of *Der bestrafte Brudermord*

No matter how many times I approach the German play titled *Der bestrafte Brudermord* ("The Punished Fratricide," which I will abbreviate as *DbB*), I come away feeling perplexed. What is it? Any serious literary discussion begins with the question of genre, and I have never been able even to classify this work: it is too grotesque to be a translation, it is not funny enough to be a parody, it is too ambitious to be a potboiler, yet its additions are all clichés. Even the subtitle of the work bothers me: *Tragœdia von Prinz Hamlet aus Dännemark*, is just inaccurate enough and just awkward enough to be grating. *Aus*, in German, indicates origin, not nobility, so the subtitle really says "Tragedy of Prince Hamlet, [who came] from Denmark." Yet in the *dramatis personae*, the Ghost is (my emphases throughout) *Geist des alten Königs von Dännemark*, ("ghost of the old king of Denmark"), with the expected word *von*.

It is a little further down in the *dramatis personae* where I am brought up short, by the name "Corambus." Now, this is a fingerprint, because Polonius is known as "Corambis" only in the 1603 or First Quarto. Albert Cohn, whose edition of *DbB* is the basis of the present study, makes much of this in his dating of the play.

> About the year 1665, this piece was performed by the Veltheim [a town in north-central Germany] company, but it is of a much older date than this, for we find it in the Dresden stage-library in 1626, and even then it was no new piece, as

there is every reason to believe that it had been brought to Germany by the English players as early as 1603.[1]

Cohn presents a wealth of source material about these actors, when and where they toured, even their salaries.   It is reasonable to believe that the English actors brought the 1603 Quarto of *Hamlet*.   Cohn stretches his facts too thin, however.   It is obvious that (the English-language) *Hamlet* is not at all the same thing as (the German-language) *DbB*.   There must have been a delay between the arrival of the Quarto in Germany and its arrival on the translator's desk, and another delay before the translation and further adaptation of the material was finished by a hand that I will call "F," for "finisher." Since the length of these delays is unknown, the date when *DbB* was actually available must also be unknown.

Cohn undercuts his own proposed dating later in his book, when he states that *DbB* "has been preserved to us only by a late and modernized copy of a much older manuscript."[2]   This statement calls his other conclusions into question: if *DbB* is preserved only in a manuscript dated "27. Oktober 1710," then the nature and even the existence of the "much older manuscript" must be nothing more than inference on Cohn's part.   Further, if the 1710 document is the earliest copy of *DbB*, then we have no way of knowing whether or not the 1626 play or the 1665 play that Cohn mentions are in fact our *DbB*. All that can be said with certainty is that Cohn has collected enormously interesting source material on the English players on the Continent shortly after 1603, and that he has published a play written no later than October, 1710.   The rest is conjecture.

Let us stick to what is on the page, even though it is a confusing mixture of wheat and chaff.   "Corambus" for Polonius indicates that *DbB* may contain other traces of the 1603 Quarto, and so we note this clue.   On the other hand, Hamlet's uncle's being named not Claudius

---

[1]   Cohn cxx

[2]   Cohn 240.

but "Erico" leads nowhere that I can see; likewise it is pointless to speculate as to why Gertrude is named "Sigrie." Yet the chaff (the post-Quarto accretions) is part of the story, and so it must be discussed along with the wheat (those parts of the play that derive from some edition of Shakespeare's *Hamlet*, to provide the reader with the basis for further analysis.

A good example of the un-Shakespearean chaff is the play's prologue. "Night" begins, *von oben* ("from above").

> *Ich bin die dunkle Nacht, die alles schlafend macht,*
> *Ich bin des Morpheus Weib, der Laster Zeitvertreib,*
> ("I am the dark night, who makes everything asleep, I am the
> wife of Morpheus, the relaxation of burdens")

Furies join her with more of this doggerel, sixteen lines in all. "Night" then switches to prose, announcing that the guilty king and queen are now consummating their marriage. "Night" will cover this sin, but she asks the Furies to scatter the sparks of revenge throughout the kingdom, *und macht der Hölle eine Freude, damit diejenige, welche in der Mord-See schwimmen, bald ersaufen; gehet, eilet, und verrichtet meinen Befehl* ("and create joy in Hell, so that these, who are swimming in a sea of murder, may soon drown; go, hasten, execute my command"). Seven more lines of doggerel end the scene.

Before beginning with the play proper, let us concentrate on a detail that may give us a clue as to the *modus operandi* of F, as I have called the adaptor or compiler who put *DbB* in its final form. The reader will have noticed that "Night" speaks *von oben* ("from above"). "Night" also ends the scene by saying, *So eilt, ich fahre auf, verrichtet euren Lauf* ("so hurry, I ascend, execute your course"). The stage directions that follow are, *Fährt auf. Musik.* ("ascends. music"). Lowering and then raising a character this way was probably not something the English players brought with them in 1603. The Elizabethan stage was amenable to some special effects, and not just sound effects: without leaving *Hamlet*, we have the Ghost under the stage crying "Swear," and the grave-digging scene in Act V, which I imagine made use of some kind of a trap door. I can think of no special effects above the stage, however. *Macbeth*'s witches may talk about hovering through fog and filthy air, but there is no evidence that they actually did any hovering onstage, nor do I know of any instance of this *Peter Pan* effect anywhere on the Elizabethan or Jacobean stage. I suspect that it would have been a difficult business on an open-air stage, but I do not know.

It is known, however, that by October of 1710 aerial effects were common in roofed theaters, thanks to Italian companies' development of what was then called "the marvelous," what we would now call special effects. As early as 1637 the inaugural opera at Venice's San Cassiano theater, Francesco Manelli's *Andromeda* had a hazardous entrance for the "Mercury" character.

> The first scene was a seascape in which Dawn, dressed in silver, appeared in a cloud. Later Juno came out in a golden chariot drawn by peacocks, and Mercury leaped from the sky in an invisible machine. Then suddenly the scene changed to a wooded pasture with snowy mountains in the background, and shortly after back to the maritime scene. Here Neptune entered in a sliver seashell drawn by four sea-horses... The other acts disclosed similar marvels.[3]

Being merely *oben* was not quite as strenuous as Mercury's entrance, but in any case it would remain an occupational hazard for German actors and singers for centuries, down to Wagner's *Tristan und Isolde* , which opens   with some poor third-string tenor, suspended somewhere *oben*, singing his solo with no orchestral accompaniment at all.

Since being *oben* is a clue that leads us to the German stage, let us follow this clue. Before unification, Germany consisted of over two

---

[3]   Palisca 120

hundred mini-states, each with a ruler and his court, and his court theater. Having two hundred-plus theaters going full-time for centuries would seem to have resulted in a strong core repertory, but all seems to have been waste and void until Goethe and Schiller arrived in the late 1700's. Put another way, two hundred-plus theaters going full-time for centuries must have resulted in a huge stockpile of bad scripts. We may never know which of these bad scripts was combined with *Hamlet* to produce *DbB*, but let us keep this mass of bad writing in mind, as a background for the model I am proposing, which is *Ariadne auf Naxos*, the opera libretto that Hugo von Hofmannsthal wrote for composer Richard Strauss. The premise of this libretto is that the impresario of a court opera has prepared a double bill, a comic farce and a heroic opera; just before curtain time he is told to combine the two pieces. The result is a very arty show that keeps the audience off-balance as it veers incongruously between the noble and the satirical.

I propose that *DbB* is the very un-arty result of just such a real-life backstage emergency, but instead of the hand of a skillful writer like von Hofmannsthal, the crisis devolved on the man I have called F, who was the undistinguished impresario of an undistinguished local theater. He is told on short notice that the local princeling has acquired a copy of *Hamlet* and wants it performed forthwith, and in German. In a panic, F goes to a courtier who has spent time in England, who paraphrases Shakespeare's play, some passages well, some passages perfunctorily. F is now in an even greater panic, because his theater has never performed so taxing a play; he knows that the princeling will hate it. He grabs a couple of old scripts from his company's library, one pseudoclassical and one knockabout, and starts cutting and pasting, adding the sort of buffoonery and breast-beating that the court audience is accustomed to.

This scenario would explain the weird variations in tone throughout *DbB*, and the *Ariadne*-like incongruities like insertion of the not-very-funny court jester named Phantasmo. This *Ariadne*-scenario would also explain why there is no *Hamlet* in the prologue, except for the (I infer) scribbled-in prose synopsis of the plot; the rest of the prologue could very well have been lifted from another play.   Should the reader object that no such play is known, or perhaps even extant, I reply that this is the same speculation that Cohn indulges in, and for that matter, that other Shakespeareans indulge in who write of an ur-*Hamlet*.   My putative ur-*DbB* is based on the common observation that some plays, dramas and comedies, do in fact fall by the wayside.   Since there is no *Hamlet* here, except for the prose patch about the wedding night of Erico and Sigrie (Claudius and Gertrude), this prologue could have been lifted from another now-forgotten play.

The play proper, Act I, scene 1, begins with another perplexing error that must be noted before dealing with the *faux* Shakespearean elements.   The sentry asks, *Was vor Freund?*   The problem is that "What <u>kind of</u> friend" is rendered with *für*, not *vor*, as in the beginning of scene 3, when the sentinel asks *Was für Runde?*   ("what kind of patrol?").   *Was vor Freund?* is literally "what <u>before</u> friend."   It is possible that *vor* for the English "for" may betray an English hand, but one word is not enough to base a scenario on.   Regardless of its source, it is safe to say that a mistake this obvious, like the *aus/von* mistake in the play's title, would be one involving haste, from which I adduce the "on short notice" part of my scenario above.   From the fact that neither mistake was corrected I adduce that the first production of *DbB* was a failure, and that it gathered dust for years until it was rediscovered by Cohn.

Much more important than this specific error, however, is the way that this opening scene immediately sets the tone of the greatest of *DbB*'s aesthetic sins, that is, being the work of a writer who had a copy of *Hamlet* before him, but didn't seem to think that the play was very good.   This would make F a predecessor of the self-important directors of our day who think that Shakespeare needs their help.   Does the Bard say, "'Tis bitter cold?"   What does the Bard know?   F has the First Sentinel say, *Ey, Camerad, es ist ja nun so kalt <u>nicht</u>.* ("Hey, buddy, it's really <u>not</u> so cold now").   Does Shakespeare let the suspense build before the ghost enters? F, perhaps with experience of the court audience's short attention-span in mind, has the unnamed Second Sentinel let the cat out of the bag straightway, and undercuts the announcement of the Ghost's appearance by treating it as slapstick. *Wisse denn, daß sich ein Gespenst an der Vorderseite des Castels sehen läßt, es hat mich schon wollen zweymal von der Bastey herunterwerfen* ("know then, that a ghost appeared on the facade of the castle, it tried to throw me down from the bastion twice"). "Healths" (a fanfare) are abruptly sounded, as the "new king" commences his revels. The Ghost wanders onstage, then wanders off again. Healths are again sounded, this time with drums, and the frightened sentry declaims, *Hätte ich doch einen Trunk Wein von des Königs Tafel, damit ich mein erschrocknes, angebranntes Herz begiessen könnte* ("if only I had a drink of wine from the king's table, so I could wet my frightened, scorched heart"), thus combining the King's rouse and the Ghost's appearance into one unfunny line.

The Ghost's second appearance combines buffoonery and what I consider the most tiresome cliché in all German literature: the *Ohrfeige*, a slap on the side of the head, what used to be called boxing someone's ears. According to the stage directions, *Geist giebt von hinten der Schildwache eine Ohrfeige, daß er die Musquete fallen läßt* ("ghost gives the sentinel a slap on the head from behind, so that he drops his musket"), and then exits again. Horatio, identified in the *dramatis personae* as "a high[-born] friend of the prince" enters, with no other purpose than to exhort the sentinel to stay awake. The ghost again wanders across the stage, and Horatio greets it with the flattest dialogue imaginable. *Bey meinem Leben, es ist ein Geist, und sieht recht ähnlich dem letztverstorbenen König von Dännemark* ("by my life, it is a ghost, and really looks like the late king of Denmark").

I have described this travesty as *faux* Shakespeare, yet it is undeniably Shakespeare, no matter how watered-down and cluttered up it may be. At times F seems to have availed himself of a good translation. After the Ghost's third appearance, Francisco observes that *Er gebehrdet sich kläglich, und läßt als ob er was sagen wollte* ("he gestured sadly, and made as if he wanted to say something"), which is very close to the original, where Horatio says (1.2.215) "yet once methought / It lifted up its head and did address / Itself to motion, like as it would speak."   We will see that transposing lines from one scene to another and from one character to another is a constant in F's method.

Now Hamlet appears, to check on the sentries, and Horatio informs him that all is well.   Then, as an afterthought, he mentions the Ghost, although he stresses its punctuality (it appears "every quarter of an hour") and the "great harm" it does to the watchmen.   Oh, and incidentally, it looks like Hamlet's late royal father.   Another flourish, as healths are drunk.   In another odd transposition, Hamlet, not Horatio, asks what the flourishes mean, and Horatio, not Hamlet, explains the revelry.   Hamlet remarks that he is somewhat bothered by his mother's hasty wedding, and that while he was in Germany, his uncle had himself crowned king of Denmark and had Hamlet made king of Norway.

With the Ghost's fourth appearance play suddenly becomes more Shakespearean again.

> Hamlet.   *Der Geist winkt mir; Ihr Herren, Sie treten ein wenig an die Seite, Horatio mache dich nicht zu weit, ich will den Geist folgen und sein Begehren*
> *vernehmen.*   *ab.*
> ("The Ghost beckons me; you gentlemen, you go off to the side a little, Horatio don't go too far off, I want to follow the Ghost and learn its desire.   [exit]")

Although this is prosy, it is at least recognizable, as is Horatio's continuation.

> Horatio.   *Ihr Herren, wir wollen ihm folgen , damit ihm kein Leid wiederfahre.*

("You gentlemen, we should follow him, so that no harm may return to him.")

The play stays on track for a while. The Ghost's account of his assassination is quite complete, and even has an original touch: *da kommt mein* <u>*Kronsüchtiger*</u> *Bruder zu mir* ("then comes my <u>crown-obsessed</u> brother to me"). Further on, though, the translation that F was using seems to have hit a rough spot.

Hamlet. *So leget Eure Finger auf meinen Degen: Wir schwören.*
      so put your fingers on   my   sword we   swear
Horat. und Francisco.   *Wir schwören.*
                          we   swear
Geist.   (*inwendig*) *Wir schwören.*
        within   we   swear

The Ghost's "Swear," instead of seconding Hamlet's command, has been diluted to a mere echo. If the stage direction *inwendig* is understood as literally "offstage" instead of "below the stage," it would mean either that the German theater could not effectively accommodate a ghost beneath the boards, or it could just as easily mean that F did not understand the (unwritten) stage direction that the Ghost be under the stage.

    F's translation for the following scene must have been more reliable, since Claudius' "Though yet of Hamlet our dear brother's death" speech is creditably summarized, except that the King gives Hamlet the choice of remaining in Denmark or going to his new kingdom, Norway. We also learn that the Laertes character (here named Leonardo, or Leonhardus in the *dramatis personae*) has already gone back to France, which has the effect of a cut: there is no Laertes-Ophelia-Polonius farewell scene.

    Instead, the action goes immediately to Hamlet's madness as revealed to Ophelia, and F's translation again fails him. Instead of the "Get thee to a nunnery" passage, Hamlet tells Ophelia a story about a bride revealing herself to her new husband without her cosmetics and her glass eye, much to the bridegroom's surprise and disappointment. Ophelia has no dialogue.   The only reference to a nunnery is with Hamlet's closing *doch, gehe nur fort nach dem Kloster, aber nicht nach einem Kloster, wo zwey Paar Pantoffeln vor dem Bette stehen* ("but just go straight to a nunnery, but not to a nunnery where two pairs of slippers are at the side of the bed").

Polonius' announcement of the actors' arrival has one oddity: "When <u>Roscius</u> was an actor in Rome" becomes *Da <u>Marus Russig</u> ein Comödiant war zu Rom.*   The 1603 Quarto reads "Rossios," which indicates that F was not working from a printed text at this point: "Rossios" can become "Russig" only through the intermediary of illegible handwriting.

As to the actors themselves, F is suddenly voluble: we learn (II.7) that they were student actors that Hamlet saw in Wittenberg, that they had hoped to perform at the recent royal wedding, that some of the student-actors on tour had left the company for engagements in Hamburg, and that they speak High (that is, Highland) German, as opposed to Low (that is, Lowland) German.   After all these additions, *DbB* again goes awry: Hamlet's speech to the players is about their wardrobe, and the play-within-a-play involves Pyrrhus' brother pouring poison in his ear.   Nevertheless, the plot goes according to plan: the King is appropriately upset.   F is unable to resist a final "tweak," however: in the confusion of the King's exit, Corambus remarks that *Die Comödianten haben einen Stumpf gemacht* ("the actors presented a flop"), which is about as far off the mark as a review could be.   True to F's gift for anticlimax, the actors ask Hamlet for a passport, and Corambus, in another out-of-sequence exchange, is told see the players well bestowed and that he should not use them according to their deserts.

DbB's Act III, scenes 1 and 2 (corresponding to Hamlet's III.3) are a competent, if prosy translation, up until the end, where the King feels better, and vows to reconcile himself to God by fasting, charitable works, and prayer.   On the other hand, the Bedroom Scene betrays many incomprehensible retouches: the Queen does not call Hamlet; Hamlet invites himself. Horatio comes into the Queen's chamber to announce Hamlet, and he sees Corambus hide behind the arras, although he evidently does not inform the Prince of this when he rejoins him offstage, since the stabbing goes on as scheduled. There is thunder and lightning as the Ghost wanders onstage and then wanders offstage again without a word. Hamlet makes a few catty remarks to the Queen, and then he too wanders off, forgetting to take the corpse of Corambus with him. The Queen expresses regret at her son's madness in a soliloquy.

The next scene is an *Ariadne* moment, as for no apparent reason, a certain Jens, a farmer, appears to pay his overdue taxes, and encounters a certain Phantasmo, a court jester. Phantasmo promises to intercede in the matter of Jens' back taxes. Ophelia enters, mad, takes Phantasmo for Hamlet, and invites the court jester to her bridal bed. She wanders off and Phantasmo exits with Jens, to clear up those back taxes.

F returns to Shakespeare's plot as Hamlet is sent to England. The scene as adapted is wordy and prolix; F has Hamlet say, *Ja, ja, König, schickt mich nur nach Portugall, auf daß ich nimmer wieder komme, das ist das beste* ("yes, yes, king, just send me to Portugal, so that I'll never come back again, that's the best"). Yet when we least expect it, there comes a moment of genuineness, although with F's trademark inaccuracy. .

> Hamlet. *Nun Adieu, Frau Mutter!*
> König. *Wie, mein Prinz, warum heist Ihr uns Frau Mutter?*
> Hamlet. *Mann und Weib is ja ein Leib, Vater oder Mutter, es*
> *ist mir gleich.*
> ("Now goodbye, Madame. Mother!" "What, my prince, why do you call us Madame Mother?" "Man and wife is indeed one body, father or mother is all the same to me.")

F veers into more low comedy, as Ophelia continues to pursue Phantasmo. To spice the action up, she strikes him, although no *Ohrfeige* is called for in the stage directions, then lapses into her lovesick delusion.

F goes lower and lower still. Hamlet has been captured by two bandits, who intend to shoot him, one standing on each side. Hamlet lurches forward, and the bandits shoot each other. What kind of audience was F writing for?

After this hilarity, we return to court, where Phantasmo has taken Corambus' place. Otherwise, the action is again Shakespearean, although perfunctory. The fencing match is agreed on, with Phantasmo taking Osric's part. F at this point evidently feels that the scene needs to be more physical.

> Hamlet.   *Sehet nur, Signora Phantasmo, es ist greulich kalt.*
> Phantasmo.   *Ja, ja, es ist greulich kalt –* [zittert mit dem Munde.
> Hamlet.   *Nun ist es schon nicht so kalt mehr.*
> Phantasmo.   *Ja, ja, es ist recht ins Mittel.*
> Hamlet.   *Aber nun ist eine große Hitze.* [wischt den Gesicht.
> Phantasmo *O welch eine greuliche Hitze!* [wischt auch den Schweiß.
>
> ("Now see, Madame Phantasmo, it is horribly cold." "Yes, yes, it is horribly cold." [his teeth chatter] "Now it's not so cold any more." "Yes, yes, it's right in the middle." "But now it's really hot" [wipes his face] "Oh, what fierce heat!" [also wipes the sweat away])

The body language continues. After Hamlet agrees to the match, he is physically shaken.

> Hamlet. *...mir fallen Blutstropfen aus der Nase; mir schüttert der ganze Leib. O wehe, wie geschiet mir.* [fällt in Ohnmacht.
>
> ("...drops of blood are falling from my nose; my whole body trembles. Oh, alas, what's happening to me." [falls unconscious.])

It appears that F regarded his unconscious Hamlet with drops of blood in his nose as the high point of the play: for the rest of the drama he appears to be just going through the motions. At the beginning of the swordfight the Queen informs the court that Ophelia has thrown herself from a cliff, but this announcement does not delay the fight. Everybody dies on schedule, and, as a bonus, Phantasmo is stabbed, too.

DbB ends as it began, with doggerel.

> *So gehts, wenn ein Regent mit List zur Kron sich dringet*
> *Und durch Verrätherey dieselbe an sich bringet,*
> *Derselb erlebet nichts, als lauter Spott und Hohn,*
> *Denn wie die Arbeit ist, so folget auch der Lohn.*
> ("That's how it is, if a prince pushes his way to the crown by trickery, and through betrayal brings it to himself, he himself experiences nothing but loud mockery and scorn, because as the work is, so the reward follows.")

The last line is a fitting epitaph for the literary oblivion of *DbB*. Except as a repository for fragments of a very early version of *Hamlet*, it holds no interest for the modern reader whatsoever.

Time and Space in the Anglo-Saxon *Seafarer*

The Old English poem *Seafarer* (*Sfr*) is preserved in the Exeter Book, an anthology presented to the Library of Exeter Cathedral not later than 1072.[1] The authorship of *Sfr* is unknown, as is its date of composition. The uncertainties do not stop there: the poem's very genre is hard to fix. It begins with a vivid description of the hardships of winter voyages on northern seas, and is therefore realistic; it continues with a sailor's reflections on the joys and sorrows of life on land, which would make it lyrical-elegiac; finally, it mixes the urge to put to sea again with the longing for a journey to a heavenly home, which is clearly homiletic.

This is a wide range of moods for a poem of only one hundred and twenty-four lines, but this paper will proceed on the assumption that the work is to be approached as it stands on the page, without the need of any clever editorial slicing and dicing. Unprejudiced reading of *Sfr* will show that the poet is quite capable of speaking for himself, and is in fact wonderfully vivid in his depictions of seascapes and wonderfully subtle in his transitions between concrete and abstract subjects. He does, however, make certain assumptions with regard to his audience, that they be familiar with the conventions of Old English poetry and with the religious world-view that he is illustrating. For this reason, it will be worthwhile to consider other Anglo-Saxon poems for context and to survey the religious outlook that was in the air at the time.

---

[1] Gordon 1

Before going beyond *Sfr*, however, let us take a closer look at what is on the page, not a micro-reading, but a mid-range view of the proportions of the poem.   Lines 1-17 describe the physical miseries of the winter voyage; 18-26 concern the psychological stress, with imagery of sea-birds; 27-47 recapitulate the themes in the context of comparison with life on land; 48-57 are a tight focus on the beauties of the earth, including the cuckoo's sad song, which is a reminder that they are ephemeral; 58-66 contrast the transitory pleasures of life on land with the sailor's life of action; the second half of the poem is a steady merging of these personal reflections with the homiletic theme of the afterlife in heaven and of understanding the greatness of God. Proportion is not the whole story; saying that *Sfr* is half one thing and half another is tantamount to saying that it is two poems, whereas the subtle interlocking of imagery and ideas between the two halves show that it is one poem.   Rather, it could be said that the first half provides the raw material of frequently-encountered Anglo-Saxon themes (longing for the good old days, the excitement of physical stress) which the poet transmutes into Christian themes in the second half. Carrying the matter of proportion further, it will be observed that the first sixty-six lines of the poem are in no way homogeneous: their content could be expressed using the musical shorthand of ABABA, or A-(sea) birds-A-(land) bird-A, which produces an aesthetically-pleasing, rounded-off fund of ideas from which the second half draws.

Ida Gordon, whose 1979 edition is the basis of the present study, discusses the matter of *Sfr*'s weighting of the realistic and the spiritual elements at length.   It is more accurate to say that she surveys previous scholars' opinions on the matter of allegory,[2] since a series of authors had approached *Sfr* with the assumption that the sea-journey is a metaphor for a life-journey or a journey of the soul.   S.A.J. Bradley's introduction to his excellent translation makes much of the similarities between *Sfr*'s philosophical outlook and those of St.

---

[2]   Gordon 14ff

Augustine in his *Confessions*.[3]   Both of these commentators'
observations are helpful to clarify the frame of mind that the modern
reader must understand to approach the homiletic parts of the poem,
but there is a risk of diminishing the impact of the first sixty-six lines
of *Sfr*, the part where the hardships of the winter voyage are
realistically and forcefully described.   Put another way, understanding
the religious works that stand behind *Sfr*, those Christian ideas that the
poet could assume that his audience would be familiar with, and which
therefore could be left unsaid, should not be the modern reader's focus.
Bradley puts it thus:

> To recognize that the *Sfr*-poet is working within an established
> Christian metaphor is surely in no way to derogate from the
> absolute quality and power of the poetry in the seafaring
> section, which stands among the finest sea-poetry in the
> language.[4]

Bradley's cautionary observations are apropos for the ending of the
poem, but not necessary for its beginning.   The modern reader
understands that when the author of *Sfr* speaks of *earfoðhwile* (time of
hardship), time is not to be understood in the misty New Age sense of
a zone of uncertainty or disorientation, but in a wide-awake, real-time
sense, where the seconds crawl by.   It is time measured in heartbeats,
in the rhythmless surge of (6) *atol yþa gewealc* ("terrible
wave-tossing"), punctuated by the stinging throb of feet that are (9)
forste gebunden / caldum clommum ("shackled in frost, gripped by
cold"), and when the narrator says that (10) *hungor innan slat /
merewerges mod* ("inner hunger tore at the sea-weary spirit"), we
understand that he is not speaking of hunger for acceptance or for
knowledge, but of the real thing.

---

[3]   Bradley 329ff
[4]   Bradley 331.

The opposite of "the real thing" in the case of *Sfr* is "the allegorical thing." The *Sfr* poet will not let the reader drift off into non-sensory ideas: he repeatedly pulls us back to the here and now by particularizing his images: not just "birds," but *ylfetu* ("swan" 19), *ganet* ("gannet" 20), *huilpan* ("curlew" 21), *earn* ("eagle" 24), *geac* ("cuckoo" 53), *mæw* ("gull") and stearn ("tern" 23). Not just "waves," but *sealtypa* ("salt-wave" 35), *atol ypa* ("terrible wave" 6) and *yða gewealc* ("tossing of the wave" 46); not just *clif* ("cliff" 8), but also *stanclif* ("rocky cliff" 23). A "color-word" like *begiellan* (screech 3) is inescapably sensory, as are color words that also particularize the image, like *isigfeþera* ("icy-feathered" 24) and *urigfeþra* ("dewy-feathered" 25).

Returning to the subject of time, the poet tells us that he has spent years in this hard life, a life beyond the comprehension of landsmen, and does so with strong sensory images.

Hu ic earmcearig	*iscealdne sæ*	
how I wretched-sorrowful	ice-cold sea	
winter wunade	*wræccan lastum*	15
winters lived	exile in-paths	
winemagum bidroren		
from-kinsmen cut-off		
bihongen hrimgicelum	*hægl scurum fleag.*	
hung with-frost-cicles	hail in-showers flew	

("how I, miserable, lived on the ice-cold sea for years, in the paths of exile, cut off from kinsmen and with icicles all around; thick hail came flying down")

Two observations need to be made here: first, the word *wræcca*, that can be understood as a wanderer or exile in a Christian sense, since a pilgrim may have an earthly destination, but that place of pilgrimage is not his home. I have spoken of line 66 as the dividing line, after which the homily starts, but understanding *wræcca* in a Christian sense is not a violation of the poem's evidently bipartite form; it is, in fact, a unifying word, in the same way that the *Sfr* poet uses a specifically nautical word, *stieran* ("steer") at 108, which has the effect of an artful echo of the literally-understood first half of the poem. The passage is worth a closer look, but before leaving *stieran* it is worth noting that this line must have had the effect of a proverb: Gordon[5] notes its similarity with line 50 of the Gnomic Verses in the Exeter Book, *Styran sceal mon strongum mode* ("a man must steer a willful heart"). Beyond this paraphrase, we note the interlocking effect of the words *healdan* ("hold fast") and *staþol* ("firm"), which are used in a concrete and a figurative sense.

> *Meotod him þæt mod <u>gestaþelað</u>, for þon he in his meahte gelyfeð.*
> Lord him that heart makes-firm for that he in his might believes
> *Stieran mon sceal strongum mode ond þæt on <u>staþelum</u> **healdan**,*
> steer man should strong heart and that on fixed hold-fast
> *ond gewis werum,   wisum clæne.   110*
> and true of-men   wise clean
> *Scyle mona gehwylc   mid gemete **healdan***
> shall man   every   with measure hold-fast
> ("The Lord will make his heart <u>firm</u>, because he has faith in his might. A man should steer the strong heart, and **hold fast** to what is <u>firm</u>, and be true to men, wise and pure. Every man should **hold fast** in moderation.")

These very literary touches are by no means unique to *Sfr*, and would not be worth mentioning were it not for the widespread belief that Anglo-Saxon poetry is primitive. Put another way, many people believe that Old English literature is not literary, a belief that has its origins in two errors: first, because the oral-formulaic theories of Parry and Lord have been mistakenly applied to these works; and second, because, since most modern readers of Anglo-Saxon verse read the combat scenes in *Beowulf* and only the combat scenes in

---

[5] Gordon 46n.

Beowulf, they assume that all of the Old English poetry that they have not read is also is like the combat scenes in *Beowulf,* or at least about combat.

(The Anglo-Saxon poet is often his own worst enemy in this respect.   Dunning and Bliss come close to the truth in the introduction to their edition of the Old English poem *Wanderer* (*Wnd*).   "The development in heroic terms of chapters xiii and xiv of [the Old English epic] *Exodus* shows another Anglo-Saxon poet's determination to have a battle of some sort even when there was no real battle in his source."[6]   I quibble with the word "determination."   Rather, I maintain that the Old English poet's characteristic vice is laziness.   Instead of the taxing business of coining idiomatic neologisms to render new concepts, with the attendant uncertainty of whether or not his audience would understand and approve of these neologisms, he often falls back on the well-worn military vocabulary that already existed in heroic poetry, and lets the formulas carry him, his narrative and his audience along.   The *Sfr* poet sins in this respect with the word *duguð* ["throng"]:   in line 80 it is the heavenly hosts, while in line 86 it is the warrior throng so familiar from heroic poetry.)

The present study is not the place to go into the details of the misapplication of Parry and Lord, but I do wish to emphasize this one instance of the damage that it has done, that is, the preconception that Old English poetry is aimless, artless and authorless, the product of centuries of random and illiterate mini-accretions, and how this preconception prevents the modern reader from seeing the rhetorically clever (and sometimes too clever) literary touches that are on the page.

An example is the passage beginning with line 103, noted by Gordon as being inspired by a verse in the book of Revelation.   If Anglo-Saxon poetry is unlearnèd, springing from the soil, as it were, then what is this learnèd reference, obviously springing from the library, doing here?   A refinement in Gordon's observation makes the point more acute.   She correctly cites Revelation 20:11 as the

---

[6]   Wanderer 95

source of this passage, "'Great is the terrible power of God, before which the earth will turn aside.' Cf. *Apocalypsis* xx.11: *a cujus conspectu fugit terra*"[7] ("from whose gaze the earth flees"). The original, however, includes the heavens as well, *et caelum*, which means that the Anglo-Saxon writer was not just inspired by a second-hand paraphrase of this verse in Revelation, but was meticulously versifying what he had accurately read first-hand.

> *Micel biþ se Meotudes egsa, for þon   hi   seo molde oncyrreð;*
> great is the of-God   awe   for that themselves the earth turn-aside
> *se gestaþelade   stiþe grundas,*
> the foundations   firm   ground
> *eorþan sceatas   ond uprodor.*   105
> earth   regions   and heaven

If the poet is supposed to be illiterate (or pre-literate, if you will), then how does he produce this versification of a source that is clearly literary?

Leaving *Sfr* momentarily, it is instructive to consider a passage on the subject of distance, or long-distance travel in the Old English epic *Andreas*. Here the Anglo-Saxon poet shows familiarity with his original, a tiresome saint's life called *Acts of St. Andrew and St. Matthew*, but he is hard-headed enough to excise elements that detract from the story. In the original, the apostle Andrew intends to go to the land of the Myrmidons to rescue Matthew. He wants to travel by sea, but needs a pilot. Poof! Who should appear to steer the boat but not just some low-level angel or other, or even a human pilot, but Jesus himself. Now, Christians believe that Jesus will come again, but they do not believe that he will come again and again and again and again and again, popping up as obligingly as a neighborhood locksmith, whenever the plot, or rather, the writer, gets stuck. The

---

[7]   Gordon 46n.

Andreas poet sensibly and confidently cuts this silly and indeed blasphemous digression.

Returning to *Sfr*, another indication of its artiness is its apparent reference to other passages in Anglo-Saxon literature.   Reference has already been made to the Gnomic Verses in the Exeter Book; also in the Exeter Book is the poem *Wnd*.   As a thought-experiment, let us imagine the following *Wnd* passage.

ðonne onwæcneð eft	*wineleas guma,*	45
then awakens again	friendless man	
gesihð him beforan	*fealwe wægas,*	
sees him before	tawny waves	
baþian brimfuglas,	*brædan feþra,*	
bathing sea-bird	spreading feathers	
hreosan hrim ond snaw	*hagle gemenged.*	
fall frost and snow	hail mixed	

("Then again the friendless man awakens, sees before him dull-colored waves, splashing sea-birds speading their feathers, falling frost and snow mixed with hail.")

I maintain that if this *Wnd* passage were inserted into the first half of *Sfr*, it would be indistinguishable from the rest of the poem. Primacy is not an issue: whether *Sfr* influenced *Wnd* or vice-versa is certainly unknowable.   Certainly observable, however, is their similarity of topic and tone, which I take to be evidence of a literary continuum.   I say literary, because it is more probable that literati (to use as vague a term as possible) would produce two stylized poems about the sea than that generations of sailors would.   On the contrary, if a sailor were to recount his memories of a sea-voyage, there would be nothing stylized about it.   One would expect the result to be like the very long passages about shipboard adventures in *Moby-Dick*. *Sfr* is not a medieval *Moby-Dick*:   the maritime passages that illustrate hardship are touched on just long enough to give us landlubbers a shudder; then they are abandoned in favor of the philosophical theme of the poem.

The same is true of *Wnd*. The *Wnd* poet gives us the same kind of shudder when he speaks of rowing laboriously over the ice-cold sea.

> *geond   lagulade   longe   sceolde*
> throughout sea-way   long   he-has-had-to
> *hreran   mid hondum   hrimcealde sæ,*
> set-in-motion   with   hand   frost-cold   sea
> *wadan wræclastas: wyrd   bið ful   aræd!*   5
> travel   paths-of-exile destiny is fully determined
> ("Throughout the seaway he has had to churn the ice-cold sea by hand, traveling the paths of exile.   Fate cannot be avoided!")

He also writes of being oppressed by anxiety in winter (25), long-ago hall scenes (29), the sailor's weary spirit on the waves (57), his longing for the good old days (58), and even the snowstorm (105) already cited.

I repeat that it is idle to speculate as to whether *Wnd* inspired *Sfr* or vice-versa, or whether either or both were inspired by a lost original. The essential point is that their similarities are evidence of a literary continuum, which means that there were Anglo-Saxon men of letters, who were aware of other Old English works besides their own.

It is equally idle to speculate as to whether the Christian content of Old English poetry came from prose homilies like sermons, or vice-versa.   It is evident that Anglo-Saxon men of letters were aware of Continental antecedents, which will bring us to our final observation on *Sfr*.

At the beginning of this paper I spoke of the difficulty of ascertaining the genre of *Sfr*, how it appears to be by turns realistic, lyrical-elegiac and homiletic.   Dunning and Bliss propose a term that includes all of these.   "We believe that the poem is an example, rather general in character, of the genre *consolatio*, and that the wisdom achieved by the *anhoga* ["solitary man"], strikingly expressed in the final lines, is the consolation the poem provides."[8]   *Consolatio* is not exactly a genre, not in the sense that realistic, lyrical-elegiac and homiletic are.   The latter three terms are trans-cultural, and accurately describe poetic responses to problems that are universal.   *Consolatio*, on the other hand, includes all three because Boethius' *Consolation of Philosophy* does, and since so many medieval writers worked with Boethius' *Consolatio* in mind, and therefore his misfortunes and his philosophy in mind, Boethius may be taken as the vanishing point beyond which an inquiry into antecedents and genre cannot go.   Thus, the question of whether distance and time in *Sfr* is really distance and time or not, is analogous to questioning Boethius' sufferings were really sufferings or not, and so on with the Anglo-Saxon narrator's retrospection and final enlightenment.

---

[8]   Wanderer 80

Schlegel's *Hamlet*

Every time I see *Hamlet* performed or reread the play, I find something new, even though it has been more than forty years since I first got to know the drama back in high school. My reading of the German translation by August Wilhelm Schlegel (1769-1845) was an especially rich vein of discoveries, because Schlegel consistently faces the difficulties of translation squarely, and his ingenuity in resolving them results in poetry whose faithfulness to the original made me see the original afresh.

The German Shakespeare Society's 1905 edition of Shakespeare's theater works is the basis of the present study. The editor's preface (dated 1898) to *Hamlet, Prinz von Dänemark* informs us that Schlegel began his translation in 1793, after *Romeo and Juliet,* and that he finished it in 1798.

A survey of Schlegel's correspondence during this period shows surprisingly few references to *Hamlet*, but there are a few passages that are worth mentioning. On May 22, 1797 he sent a draft of an unspecified Shakespeare translation to Christoph Martin Wieland (1733-1813), who had preceded him as a translator of twenty-two of Shakespeare's plays into German between 1762 and 1766. This homage was generous, given the contemporary attacks on Wieland by younger writers, because, in the assessment of literary scholar Ken Larson, "as the most successful writer of the previous generation, [Wieland's] star had to fall before theirs could rise."[1] Schlegel gives Wieland his due as the man *der unsre Nation zuerst mit Shakespeare*

---

[1] Larson, website

bekannt machte ("who first introduced our nation to Shakespeare").[2]
Before leaving Schlegel's letters, it is amusing to note that a year later,
in a letter to a friend, on the subject of his translation of *Romeo and
Juliet*, that, *Ich hoffe, sie werden in Ihrer Schrift unter anderem
beweisen, Shakespeare sei kein Engländer gewesen.   Wie kam er nur
unter die frostigen, stupiden Seelen auf dieser brutalen Insel?*[3] ("I
hope you will note among other things in your writing, that
Shakespeare has not become an Englishman.   How did he wind up
among the frosty, stupid souls of this brutish island?")   He closes the
letter with a detailed scorn for English critics that shows that Schlegel
was up to date on his secondary sources as well as his primary ones.
From the general to the specific, in his essay "*Shakespeare und
Wilhelm Meister*," he calls attention to today's topic.   *Hamlet ist von
jeher vielleicht das bewunderste und gewiß das mißvertandenste unter
allen Stücken Shakespeares gewesen.*[4]   ("*Hamlet* is in the long run the
most admirable and certainly the most misunderstood among all of
Shakespeare's works.")   This paucity of references to Schlegel's own
Hamlet is just as well, since the focus of the present essay is the
straight-across comparison of the translation and Shakespeare's
original.

It may be said at the outset that Schlegel deals successfully with
the translation problems, but that his approach is flexible: sometimes
it is literal, at other times accurate in sense but idiomatic in German;
there are times when the necessity of rhyme calls for poetic license, as
with Hamlet's exuberant "stricken deer" jingle after "The Mousetrap."
Besides his demonstrable fidelity and ingenuity, as I have stated above,
there are moments where Schlegel's renderings are a revelation to an
English speaker, helping him see what is on the page more clearly.
This mix of different kinds of excellence, sometimes definable and
sometimes elusive, does not lend itself to the chronological explication

---

[2]   Schlegel 1962, 30
[3]   Schlegel 1962, 42.
[4]   Schlegel 1974, 55.

of a scene-by-scene overview, so I ask the reader's indulgence as I discuss the beauties of Schlegel's achievement in no particular order.

Regardless of the lack of a master plan, however, I do begin at the beginning, with the very first exchange in the play (my emphases throughout).

> Bernardo. *Wer da?*
> who there
> Francisco. *Nein, m i r antwortet: steht und gebt Euch kund.*
> no   me   answer   stand and give yourself known
> ("Who's there?"   "No, answer *me*:   stand and declare yourself.")

All is workmanlike, although "declare yourself" does not have the unexpected content of Shakespeare's "unfold yourself." Schlegel editorializes very slightly, however, on the word *mir*: the extra spaces between the letters are the equivalent of italics in English. Thus, the translator very appropriately guides the reader directly to the nuance of "I won't answer *you*; you answer *me*," by his orthography.

Craftsmanship and polish, however, are not always enough. Rhyme is a parameter that puts extra demands on the translator. I have cited Hamlet's wild "stricken deer" quatrain earlier; I confess that in the first draft of this essay I wrote "Hamlet's wild singing," although there is no indication that Hamlet sings these lines. The verses do have a crude musicality, however, and Schlegel does them justice. He omits Shakespeare's deer, however.

> *Ei, der Gesunde hüpft und lacht,*
> oh the healthy-one hops and laughs
>   *Dem   Wunden   ist's   vergällt;*
>   s-for-the injured   is-it   embittered
> *Der eine schläft, der andre wacht,*
> the   one sleeps   the other stays-awake

> *Das ist der Lauf der Welt.*
> that is the course of-the world

("Hey, the healthy one hops around and laughs, the injured one is embittered.   The first one sleeps, the other one stays awake.   That's the way the world goes.")

The word *vergällt* ("embittered") is literally "galled," which will have an aesthetically pleasing echo when Rosenkrantz and Guildenstern come to Hamlet after "The Mousetrap" with the news that the king is "marvelous distempered."

> Hamlet.   *Vom Trinken, Herr?*
>   from   drink   sir
> Güldenstern.   *Nein, vom Galle.*
>   no   from gall
> ("From drinking, sir?"   No, from gall.")

"Choler" is in fact *Galle*, so this echo of *vergällt* is the result of Schlegel's fidelity to the original.

It may be noted in passing that the German Shakespeare Society's editor uses the word *hüpfen* ("hop around," as above) to gloss Schlegel's rendering of   "the swaggering upspring:"[5]   *Hüpftanz* for Schlegel's "waltz."   More fully, the passage is *Der König wacht die Nacht durch, zecht vollauf, / Hält Schmaus und taumelt <u>den geräusch'gen Walzer</u>*; ("The king stays up all night, guzzles a lot, holds a banquet and staggers through <u>the raucous waltz</u>.")   Perhaps it would be better to say that the editor updates Schlegel's word: the waltz in 1798 had none of the refinement that it would later acquire at the hands of Chopin (1810-1849) and Strauss (father and son, 1804-1849 and 1825-1899 respectively).   In Europe in 1798 the minuet still held sway, and when that stately dance finally gave ground,

---

[5]   *Werke* 148

it would not be to the waltz, but to the more dynamic, but still very poised polonaise. The semantic root of the word waltz, after all, means "roll around" or even "wallow." The Elsinore waltz would thus have been be "raucous," not elegant. The 1898 editor was simply restoring the original connotations of coarseness by suggesting the grotesque-sounding *Hüpftanz* ('hop-around dance") in its place.

Before leaving this passage (to pick up the "stricken deer" thread), let us note an example of what I will call re-sensitizing the text. For an English speaker, at least for me, "reels" in a dance context is a dead word, or at least a word lacking ambiguity: "reel" in modern English is a specific kind of dance tune, lively, yet decorous, in the hornpipe-jig-clog-square-dance family, and that is that. When I found Schlegel's rendering *taumeln* ("stagger, be giddy"), I was reminded of the ambiguity of what Hamlet is actually saying: the king is dancing, but clumsily, drunkenly.

Let us return to the question of how Schlegel deals with the parameter of rhyme, proceeding from "the stricken deer" to "Damon dear."

> *Denn dir, mein Damon, ist bekannt*
> then to-you my Damon it-is known
> *Dem Reiche   ging zu Grund*
> as-for-the kingdom went to ground
> *Ein Jupiter: nun herrschet hier*
> a   Jove   now rules   here
> *Ein rechter, rechter – Affe.*
> a   true   true   ape
> Horatio.   *Ihr hättet reimen können.*
> you had   rhyme   can
> ("For it is known to you my Damon, that the kingdom's Jove perished.Now rules here a true, true – ape." "You could have rhymed.")

It is a pleasing coincidence that Schlegel's presumed rhyme can be translated straight across: "ground" rhymes with "hound."   In German, however, *Hund* is a strong insult, so Shakespeare's "was"/ (presumably) "ass" rhyme is mirrored precisely in intensity by *Grund /* (presumably) *Hund.*

Schlegel is his own best commentator here.   In *Von der Wirkung des Reims* ("on the operation of rhyme"), a lecture he delivered in 1798, he said, *Der große Zauber des Reims ist aus dem beständigen Wechsel erregter und befriedigter Erwartung sehr erklärbar.   Man kann sagen,daß jeder neue Reim in einem Gedichte eine Art von aufgegebenem Rätsel ist.*[6]   ("The great magic of rhyme is quite explicable by the constant alternation of stimulated and relieved expectation.   One can say that every new rhyme in a poem is a kind of posed riddle.")

Schlegel is frequently confronted with the question of how to render "thou" or "you."   Shakespeare is not always consistent: at times he seems to be playing a restless sort of grammatical cat-and-mouse.   Returning to the opening scene, Bernardo first says, "get thee to bed, Francisco," and then "Have you had a quiet guard?" German, on the other hand, is more consistent: *du* is intimate, direct, while *ihr* is respectful, distant, proper, when it is not "you (plural)." Crossing from one pronoun to the other is a great divide, not only for intimacy, but for grammar: the imperative forms of the verb reflect this distinction.   Thus, a simple line like Bernardo's "Sit down awhile," involves a decision on the translator's part: is the request comradely, or courtly?

An English speaker is prone to read right over this distinction. For him, "thou" is first and foremost an old form of "you," and normally nothing more; or, if any distinction exists, it is a completely backwards distinction based on a faulty understanding of the word's use in the Authorized ("King James") Version of the Bible: that is, if "thou" is used with God Almighty, then "thou" must be an

---

[6]   Schlegel 1989, 46

augmentative, a word to convey grandeur. Quite the contrary is true, of course, but old habits die hard. It is helpful to step away from English for perspective on what is really on the page.

The first instance we will address is vivid, because it is comical. In the opening scene, Horatio is addressed formally, until the Ghost appears. Then gentility goes out the window, and the *du*-forms of the verbs and pronouns produce just the right touch of panic.

> Marcellus.   *<u>Du bist</u> gelehrt, <u>sprich du</u> mit ihm, Horatio.*
>   you are learnèd speak you with him Horatio
> Bernardo.   *Sieht's nicht dem König gleich?   <u>Schau's an</u>, Horatio.*
>   looks it not   the   king   like   look it at   Horatio
> ("<u>You are</u> educated.   <u>You talk</u> to it, Horatio."   "Doesn't it look like the king?   <u>Look at it</u>, Horatio.")

After the Ghost departs, they regain their composure and resume their courtly, poised discourse.

> Bernardo.   *Wie nun, Horatio!   <u>Ihr zittert</u> und <u>seht</u> bleich.*
>   how now Horatio   you tremble and look   pale
> ("How now, Horatio?   <u>You tremble</u> and <u>look</u> pale.")

An example of *du/ihr* that is not at all comical, but psychologically revealing, is Hamlet's exchange with Rosenkrantz and Guildenstern, beginning with their meeting in Act II, scene 2.

> Hamlet. *Meine trefflichen guten Freunde! Was <u>machst du</u>, Güldenstern?*
>   my   excellent good friends   what do you Guildenstern
> ("My excellent good friends!   <u>How are you</u>, Guildenstern?")

Contrast this with the continuation of the "choler" passage cited above. Instead of the forthright *du*, appropriate for childhood friends, there is the arch ambiguity of *ihr*: Hamlet could be referring to both of them, ("you, plural"), or it could mean that they have been grammatically "demoted," so that they are no longer granted the confidential and trusted *du* status.

> Hamlet.   *Ihr solltet mehr gesunden Verstand beweisen...*
>   You   had   more   sound   understanding shown
> ("You would have shown sounder understanding...")

Then Hamlet resolves the ambiguity by the singular.

> Hamlet.   *Ich bin zahm, Herr, sprecht!*
>   I   am tame   sir   speak
> ("I am tame, sir.   Speak.")

Not Bernardo's spontaneous *sprich*, but the coldly formal *sprecht*. Rosenkrantz and Guildenstern have been demoted.   By contrast, in the same scene, Horatio is promoted.   When he first appears, Hamlet greets him formally.

> Hamlet. *Mein guter Freund; vertauscht mir jenen Namen.*
>   my   good   friend exchange   me   that   name
> *Was macht ihr   hier von Wittenberg, Horatio?*
> what   do you   here from Wittenberg Horatio
>   ("My good friend; exchange that name with me.   What are
> you doing here away from Wittenberg, Horatio?")

Was macht ihr? is exactly the same as the earlier *Was machst du, Güldenstern?,* except for the tone, the level of intimacy.   After Hamlet's address to the traveling players, the audience finds that a change has taken place.

> Hamlet.   *Du bist grad' ein so wackrer Mann, Horatio,*
>   you are   just   a   so   brave   man   Horatio
> *Als je mein Umgang einem mich verbrüdert.*
> as ever my association to-one me fraternized

Horatio. *Mein bester Prinz –*
      my   best   prince

Hamlet. *Nein, <u>glaub'</u> nicht daß ich schmeichle.*
      no believe   not   that I   flatter
("<u>You are</u> as stout-hearted a man, Horatio, as ever my associations have led me to be intimate with." "My dear prince..." "No, don't <u>believe</u> that I'm flattering you.")

I repeat that an English speaker's tendency would be to read right over these thou/you distinctions, thereby losing nuances that the Bard has put in.   In both of the instances cited above, in fact, Shakespeare has the thou/you distinctions, but they seem clearer in German.   A final, nuance-rich example from the Bedroom Scene:

Hamlet. *Nun, Mutter, was gibt's?*
     now   mother   what   is-it
Königin. *Hamlet, <u>dein</u> Vater ist von <u>dir</u> beleidigt.*
queen   Hamlet your   father is by you offended
Hamlet. *Mutter, mein Vater ist von <u>Euch</u> beleidigt.*
     mother   my   father is by you   offended
Königin. *<u>Kommt, kommt! Ihr sprecht</u> mit einer losen Zunge...*
     come   come   you speak with a loose tongue
("Now, mother, what is it?"   "Hamlet, <u>your</u> father is offended by <u>you</u>."   "Mother, my father is offended by <u>you</u>." "<u>Come, come!   You speak</u> with a loose tongue...")

This grammatical ping-pong continues until Gertrude uses the *du* of panic noted earlier.

Königin. *Was <u>willst du</u> thun? <u>Du willst</u> mich doch nicht morden?*
     what will you do   you will me   then not   murder
("What do <u>you want</u> to do? Do <u>you</u> not <u>wish</u> to murder me, then?")

I close with a disconnected sampling of Schlegel's renderings. "Not a mouse stirring," is charmingly translated, *"Alles mausestill,"* ("everything mouse-quiet"). How does he translate "It out-Herods Herod?" Tamely: *übertyrannt den Tyrannen* ("it over-tyrants the tyrant"). Polonius' account of his amateur acting career?

> *...ich ward auf dem Kapitol umgebracht; Brutus brachte mich um.*
>   I   was in   the   Capitol   killed   Brutus   killed   me
> Hamlet. *Es war brutal von ihm, ein so kapitales Kalb umzubringen.*
>   it was brutal of him   a   such capital calf   to-kill
> ("I was killed in the Capitol.   Brutus killed me."   "It was brutal of him to kill such a capital calf.")

"Metal more attractive?" *Hier ist ein stärkerer Magnet* ("Here is a stronger magnet"). My final example is another instance of Schlegel's resensitizing the text for me. Ever since I first got to know the drama back in high school, I had always taken "as easy as lying" in the same sense as "shall I lie in your lap," that is, amatory. Schlegel chooses otherwise: *Es ist so leicht wie lügen.* "It is as easy as lying," but lying in the sense of prevaricating. Shakespeare wrote an ambiguous word; Schlegel had to choose one sense or the other, since the German words for each sense are distinct. In making his choice, however, he gave me, the English-speaking reader, a reminder of yet another nuance in this very rich text.

Comical Barbarians

The Latin word *barbarus* is understood to be a loan-word, from the Greek ΒΑΡΒΑΡΟΣ, (barbáros) whose root meaning seems to have been "jabbering." "Bar-bar" can be understood as onomatopoeia, equivalent to "yack-yack," or speech that is unintelligible (to a Greek). The great Liddell & Scott *Greek-English Lexicon* informs us[1] that ΒΑΡΒΑΡΟΣ is not found in Homer, but ΒΑΡΒΑΡΟΦΩΝΟΣ ("barbaróphōnos," the "phōn-" being the same as in the English "phonic," and so "yack-yack speaking") does occur in the *Iliad* (2.867), where it refers to the Carians. It is a small jump from "not speaking Greek" to "not intelligent enough to speak Greek," and so the pejorative sense of the word was established early on. As a loan-word it arrived in Rome early on: the Oxford Latin Dictionary shows that *barbarus* occurs in the fragments of the earliest Latin authors whose works have come down to us: in Ennius, Pacuvius, Naevius and Caecilius.[2] The Latin word had much the same semantic range as the English "barbarian" or "barbaric." It could mean uncivilized or cruel. This essay will focus on a more specialized meaning of the word, another definition in the Oxford Latin Dictionary: "A foreigner from a Greek standpoint, a non-Greek; in Roman use, one other than a Greek or Roman." From an artistic standpoint, this is a fruitful inconsistency, since cosmopolitan Rome was both Greek and Roman, having a large population from the Greek cities of southern Italy (*magna Graecia*, "greater Greece") as well as immigrants from

---

[1] L&S 306b, s.v.
[2] OLD 225b, s.v.

Greece proper; in a theater audience we may infer that there would be comedic possibilities in the ambiguity of the word.   A Roman theatergoer would think of *barbarus* as referring to faraway places with strange-sounding names, while a Greek would apply the word to the Roman sitting next to him; the Phoenician in the next row would apply it to himself, and each would be aware of what the other was thinking.   All three would react to incongruous juxtapositions of Greek and Latin references.   The wily slave Epidicus in the comedy of that name by Titus Maccius Plautus (d. 184 B.C.) presents just such a jumble as he theatrically moans and groans about how hard he has been looking for old Periphanes.   (My emphases throughout.)

> Epidicus: *di immortales, utinam conveniam domi*   196
> immortal gods, if-only I could find at home
> *Periphanem, per omnem urbem quem sum defessus quaerere:*
> Periphanes, for whom I've worn myself out looking all over town:
> *per medicinas, per tonstrinas, <u>in gymnasio atque in foro</u>,*
> through drugstores, barbershops, <u>in the gymnasium and in the forum...</u>

The ΓΥΜΝΑΣΙΟΝ (gymnásion, "an enclosed place for physical and mental exercise") was a quintessentially Greek institution, while the outdoor forum was quintessentially Roman.   Plautus has another juxtaposition in the next line:

> *per   <u>myropolia</u>   et lanienas circumque   argentarias.*
> through <u>perfume-shops</u> and butchers and-all-around moneylenders

Myropolium is plainly the Greek ΜΥΡΟΠΩΛΙΟΝ (myropólion, as in the English "myrrh"), while the butchers' and moneylenders' quarters were well-known Roman landmarks.

   The topic of this essay will be the use of the word and the concept of *barbarus* for comic effect in *Epidicus* and five other plays by

Plautus (*Mr. Weevil, A Little Box, Casina, Hostages*, and *The Menaechmus Twins*).

Having "comic" and "Plautus" in the same sentence is redundant. Paraphrasing a modern writer,[3] Plautus was not the last of the Romans; he was the first of the Italians.   If he ever wrote a serious line, I have never encountered it.   Verbal razzle-dazzle was his specialty, and he seems to be striving for a laugh in every line.   The effect is a free-wheeling hilarity that builds and builds throughout the play, where the modern reader, and, we infer, the ancient audience, begins to expect that any word can lead to a joke.

To establish a baseline, let us consider examples that are purely Latin.   Both are from *Casina*.   First, an unexpected internal rhyme:

Myrrina.   *Tace sis, stulta, et mi ausculta.* 204
Be quiet, you dummy, and pay attention to me.

Next, a brainless-sounding repetition of *mal-* ("bad").

Lysidamus. *Tace.*
Be quiet.
Olympio.   *Non taceo.*
I won't be quiet.
Lys.   *Quae res?*
What's the matter?
Oly.   *Mala malae male monstrat.*   826
The bad lady's giving the bad girl bad advice.

Earlier in *Casina* we find

Oly. *Aha, hodie –*   726
Lys.   *Mane vero...*

---

[3]   Ogilvie 24

Hodie means "today;" *mane* is a pun: it can mean, "wait," but it can also mean "in the morning."   Thus,

> Olympio: Aha!   Today...
> Lysidamus: Wait a minute...

Or

> Olympio: Aha!   Today...
> Lysidamus: No, tomorrow...

If a humdrum word like *mane* is played for laughs, then we may take it that a resonant, colorful word like *barbarus* was supposed to be at least as funny to Plautus' original audience.

> Oly.   *sed lepide nitideque volo, nil moror barbarico bliteo.* 747
> But an elegant, splendid [meal] I want; I-won't-put-up with-barbarian mush.

This may have resonated with expatriate Greeks homesick for Greek cuisine.

Time was when it was customary to dismiss Plautus' audience out of hand as a boorish rabble, barbarians in the modern sense of the word, by taking at face value a passage in Terence (d. 159B.C.), the other Roman comic playwright whose works have survived to our day, to the effect that he twice lost an audience to nearby circus acts.[4]   Instead of uncritically taking Terence at his word, let us examine the internals of Plautus' plays.   The laugh reveals the laugher.   True, there is nothing highbrow at all about Plautus' onstage gimmicks: they involve slapstick, buffoonery and mistaken identity; his dialogue is full of doubletalk and dirty jokes.   Yet when we look closer we will not find anything really lowbrow, either.   The fact that Plautus makes jokes in

---

[4]   Hecyra 39ff

Greek means that his audience must have understood some Greek, although Palmer points out an important qualifying nuance:

> It should be realized that most of the numerous Greek loan-words found in the Latin at this period were not introduced by the educated classes. There can be little doubt that many of them were picked up by the Roman plebs in their intimate contact with Greeks who had settled in the city, and formed an integral part of the everyday speech of the lower strata of the population. This is strongly suggested by the fact that in the plays of Plautus Greek words and expressions occur predominantly in the passages spoken by slaves and low characters.[5]

Continuing the scene from *Casina*, we find

> Lys. *Quae res?*   729
> ("What's the matter?")
> Oly. *Haec res.   etiamne adstas?   enim vero*
> ("This is the matter.   Haven't you gone yet?   Because you're really
> ΠΡΑΓΜΑΤΑ ΜΟΙ ΠΑΡΕΧΕΙΣ[6]
> giving me a headache.")
> Lyc.   *Dabo tibi* ΜΕΓΑ ΚΑΚΟΝ[7]
> ("I'll give you a big headache,
> *ut ego opinor, nisi   resistis.*
> I think, unless you stand still.")

After punctuating the scene with a final Grecism, then a vulgar pun on *vomere* ("vomit, burst out in rage"), Plautus can't resist a final comedic "kick," a repetition of the *hodie/mane* quibble cited earlier.

---

[5]   Palmer 83
[6]   (prágmatá moi parékheis)
[7]   (méga kakón)

Oly.   Ω ZEY.[8]
("Good Lord!
potin a me abeas, nisi me vis vomere hodie.
beat it, won't you, unless you want me to-explode/vomit today.")
Lys. *Mane.*
("Tomorrow/wait.)

The audience must also have understood some Punic, the language of the Phoenicians and the Carthaginians: in a comedy not within the scope of this paper, *Poenulus* ("The Guy from Carthage"), there is a very long Punic-to-Latin mistranslation shtick at the beginning of Act V; there is no record of the audience wandering off to see a circus act, so we may infer that they found it not only intelligible, but entertaining.[9]

Plautus, always unpredictable, treats these non-Roman spectators in a variety of ways. At times a foreign word appears for no apparent reason at all. It is an open question as to how naturalized the Greek interjection BABAI (babaí, "wow!") or its cousin ΠΑΠΑΙ (papaí) was, or how carefully the Romans observed the slight semantic nuance that each conveyed (BABAI being surprise or disbelief, while ΠΑΠΑΙ could carry an undertone of chagrin). Just to be sure, Plautus serves up both. To render the exoticness of the word, I use a well-known Spanish interjection.

Cleost. *Quid?* 906
("What?")
Oly.   *Babae.*
("¡Ay-ay-ay!")
Cleost.   *Quid?*
Oly.   *Papae.*
("¡Ay-ay-ay-ay-ay!")

---

[8] (Ô zdêu)
[9] Skupin 1990, *passim.*

It is likewise an open question as to how exotic the word *tessera* (*A Little Box* 153) was in Plautus' time.   *Tessera* was a sort of Roman credit card or calling card, a "chip" made of stone or porcelain; the word would seem to be derived from the Greek ΤΕΣΣΕΡΑΓΟΝΟΣ (tesserágonos) or ΤΕΤΡΑΓΟΝΟΣ (tetrágonos), literally "four-angled."

There is no doubt about the exoticness of this passage from *Hostages,* however.   After swearing by Apollo, the parasite Ergasilus swears by a series of Roman cities – in Greek.

> Hegio.   *Et captivum illum Alidensem?*
> and hostage   that   of-Elis
> Ergasilus.   ΜΑ ΤΟΝ ΑΠΟΛΛΟΝ.[10]
>   yes   by   Apollo
> Heg.   *Et servolum*   880
>   and   slave
> *meum Stalagmum, meum qui gnatum surripuit?*
> my   Stalagmus   my   who   son   stole
> Erg.   ΝΑΙ ΤΑΝ ΚΟΠΑΝ[11]
>   yes   by   Cora

Here Plautus pivots.   Following Apollo by Cora is logical, since Cora could be the Doric Greek word ΚΟΡΑ (kóra), corresponding to the more common ΚΟΡΗ (kórē).   Both words mean "daughter," but are commonly used as a euphemism for Persephone, the daughter of Demeter and queen of Hades.   Plautus seizes on another ambiguity, however: there was an Italian city named Cora, and so the playwright veers into a series of oaths where Italian towns are sworn by.

> Heg.   *Iam   credo?*
> already   I-believe

---

[10] Ma ton Apollon
[11] Nai tan Koran

Erg.   ΝΑΙ ΤΑΝ ΠΡΑΙΝΕΣΤΕΝ[12].
          yes   by   Praeneste
Heg.   *Venit?*
                           he-come
Erg.   ΝΑΙ ΤΑΝ ΣΙΓΝΙΑΝ[13]
                                 yes   by   Signia
Heg. *Certon?*
     for-sure?
Erg.   ΝΑΙ ΤΟΝ ΦΡΟΥΣΙΝΟΝΑ [14]
          yes   by   Phrousino
Heg.   *Vide   sis.*
                           watch you-should
Erg.   ΝΑΙ ΤΟΝ ΑΛΑΤΡΙΟΝ.[15]
                                 yes   by   Alatrium

("H.   And the hostage from Elis?   E.   Yes, by Apollo.   H.   And
my slave Stalagmus, who stole my son?   E.   Yes, by Cora (the
goddess or the town).   H.   Already, I believe?   E. Yes, by Praeneste.
H.   Coming?   E.   Yes, by Signia.   H.   For sure?   E.   Yes, by
Phrousino.   H.   You'd better watch it.   E.   Yes, by Alatrium.")

     Then comes the "kicker:"   old Hegio identifies these Italian
cities as "barbarian," and Ergasilus' reply recalls his brother-parasite
Epidicus' loathing of   "barbarian mush."

     Heg.   *Quid   tu   per barbaricas urbes iuras?*
            why   you   by barbarian   cities   swear?
     Erg.   *Quia enim item asperae*
                                because for same harsh

---

[12] Nai tan Prainesten
[13] Nai tan Signian.
[14] Nai ton Phrousinona.
[15] Nai ton Alatrion.

sunt ut tuom victum autumabas esse.
are as   your   food you-claim   to-be
Heg.   *Vae aetati tuae!*
                                  alas   age   your
("H.   Why   are   you   swearing   by   barbarian   cities?   E.
Because they   set   my   teeth   on   edge,   just   as   you   say   your
banquet will.   H.   You're shameless.")

Zany Greek names are a trademark of Plautus, and so become an inside
joke to his Greek-speaking audience.   Mr. Weevil announces that he
has come

> Curculio.   *ab Therapontigono Platagidoro milite*   408
>   from Therapontigonos Platagidoros soldier

The *thera-* part of the name means "companion," often in a military
sense.   I am unable to improve on Nixon's rendering of the full name:
Captain Therapontigonus Smackahead.[16]

> Lyco.   *Novi   edepol nomen, nam mihi istoc nomine,*
>   I-know by-George name for to-me by-that name
> *dum scribo , explevi totas   ceras   quattuor.*   410.
> while I-write I-filled   all   wax-sheets   four
> ("By George, I know that name.   Just writing it down took up
> four pages of my notebook.")

Nor does Plautus let up, describing the Captain's exploits in countries
known, unknown and unheard-of.

> Lyc.   *Quam ob rem istuc?*   442
>   [a monument] for what

---

16 Nixon 233

Cur.   *Dicam.   quia enim Persas, Paphlagones,*
              I'll-tell because *Persians Paphlagonians*
Sinopes, Arabes, Cares, Cretanos, Syros,
Sinopeans Arabs Carians Cretans Syrians
Rhodiam atque Lyciam, Perediam et Perbibesiam,
Rhodes and   Lycia   Eatitup-ia and Drinkitdown-ia
Centauromachiam et Classiam Vnomammiam,
Centaurfight-ia   and   Onebreastfleet-ia
Libyamque oram omnem, omnem Conterebromniam,
Libya-and coast   all   all   Stompthegrape-ia
dimidiam partem nationum usque omnium
   half   part of-nations up-to   of-all
subegit   solus   intra   viginti dies.
he-conquered by-himself inside-of twenty   days
("A monument for what?"   "I'll tell you.   Because he
single-handedly conquered the Persians, the Paphlagonians,
the Sinopeans, Arabians, Carians, Cretans, Syrians, Rhodes
and Lycia and Eatitup-ia and Drinkitdown-ia, Centaurfight-ia
and Onebreastfleet-ia, the whole coast of Lib-i-a, all of
Stompthegrape-ia, all in under twenty days.")

In the prologue to *Casina* the non-Roman spectators are "in the know,"
and it is the Latin-speaking Romans that have to be informed as to the
"barbarian" slave rights on which the plot of the comedy turns.

Sunt   hic, inter se quos nunc credo dicere:
There-are-those here to each other who now I-think are-saying
"quaeso, hercle, quid istuc est?   serviles nuptiae?
   I-ask   by-George what this is slave weddings
servin   uxorem   ducent   aut   poscent sibi?
slaves a-bride lead-down-the-aisle or propose-to for-themselves
novom   attulerunt,   quid   fit nusquam gentium."
a-novelty   they-come-up-with which exists nowhere   on-earth

at ego aio id   fieri   in Graecia et Carthagini,
but   I   say   it is-the-case in   Greece and Carthage
et   hic in nostra terra in Apulia;
and here in our land, in Puglia (southern Italy, *magna Graecia*)
id   ni   fit,   mecum   pignus si quis   volt   dato
(if) that's not the-case with-me a-wager if anybody wants-to   give
in urnam   mulsi,   Poenus   dum   iudex   siet
in a-big-cup of-sweetened-wine so-long-as the-judge is a-Carthaginian
vel Graecus adeo, vel mea causa   Apulus.
or   a-Greek then   or in-my defense   a-Puglian
quid nunc?   nihil agitis?   sentio, nemo sitit.
what now   nothing you-do   I-get-it nobody's thirsty
("There are those among us, I'm sure, who are asking each
other, 'What's this?   Slave weddings?   Slaves getting
married   or   popping   the   question?   They're   claiming
something never heard of on land or sea.'   But I'm here to
tell you that this does happen in Greece and Carthage, and
even here in our own southern Italy.   If you don't think so,
let's bet a big cup of honeyed wine, so long as the judge is a
Cathaginian, or a Greek, or even a southern Italian.   Well
now, no takers?   I get it; nobody's thirsty.")

Here the Greeks and Carthaginians must have been nodding wisely and
winking at each other as the Roman spectators are brought up to date.
Not bad, for a ΒΑΡΒΑΡΟΣ.   Plautus understands us.   Plautus is on our
side.

Later in the same play, "Attic" is used as a symbol of probity.
                    Scibis,   audi.   648
                    You-will-know listen
malum pessimumque hic modo intus apud nos
bad   and-the-worst here just-now inside in the house
tua   ancilla   hoc pacto exordiri coepit,
your maidservant   thus   set-off   began

quod haud Atticam condecet   disciplinam.
what scarcely Attic   was-fitting civilized-behavior
("You'll find out.   Listen.   It was bad, worse than bad just
now, in our home, your maidservant started acting in a way
contrary to Attic decorum.")

In point of fact, however, a Greek setting, whether in Greece itself or
in the overseas colonies, was a given.   In *Casina* (81) the ingénue
invenietur et pudica et libera, / ingenua Atheniensis ("will be found to
be chaste and free-born / the daughter of an Athenian citizen"), and in
Epidicus (53) the young man *id adeo argentum ab danista apud*
Thebas sumpsit faenore ("borrowed this money from a loan-shark in
Thebes at interest").   Both settings are gratuitous.   Plautus spells this
out in the prologue to *The Menaechmus Twins.*

Atque hoc poetae faciunt in comoediis:
and   thus authors   do   in   comedies
omnis res gestas esse Athenis autumant,
all things done be in-Athens they-allege
quo   illud vobis graecum videatur magis;
by-which it   to-you   Greek   may-seem more
ego nusquam dicam   nisi   ubi   factum dicitur.   10
I   nowhere will-say unless   where   done   is-said
atque adeo hoc argumentum graecissa ,   tamen
and   thus this   tale   is-Greek-ified,   but
non atticissat, verum sicilicissitat.
not Attic-ified   in-fact Sicily-fied
("And   authors   do   this   in   comedies.   All   the   action,   is
supposed to be in Athens, which is supposed to make it seem
more Greek to you.   I won't say that the setting is anywhere
other than where it's said to be, and so the story is Greek-ified,
not Attic-ified, but in fact Sicily-fied.")

In my mind's eye I see the Greeks in the audience nudging each other: Yes, Plautus may be a ΒΑΡΒΑΡΟΣ , but he's on our side.   Still later in the play, however, in the middle of the buffoonery of a cross-dressing mistaken-identity shtick, the very virile slave disguised as a girl asks,

> Chalinus. *Ubi tu es, qui colere mores Massilienses postulas?* 963
> where you are who cultivate manners of-Marseilles propose
> ("Where are you, who are intending to cultivate Marseilles manners?")

Marseilles was proverbial for licentiousness,[17] but it was a Greek colony.   Is Plautus really on our side?

At other times, the Greeks in the audience must have winced.   In *Mr. Weevil* the title-role parasite is in a hurry, talking loudly about how he'll push people out of his way.   The people he's going to push out of the way have appropriate local-color Greek titles: *nec strategus nec tyrannus quisquam, nec agoranomus, / nec demarchus nec comarchus* ("no general nor chief at all, no market-inspector / nor alderman nor commissioner").   Yet even when his rambling diatribe becomes anti-Greek, the speaker cannot express himself without using Greek words: ΘΕΡΜΟΠΩΛΙΟΝ (thermopólion, "a place where hot drinks are sold," on the analogy of ΜΥΡΟΠΩΛΙΟΝ mentioned earlier), and ΔΡΑΠΕΤΗΣ (drapétēs, "renegade").

> Curculio. *tum isti Graeci palliati, capite operto qui ambulant,* 288
> then those Greeks robed, with-heads wrapped-up who walk-around
> *qui incedunt suffarcinati cum libris, cum   sportulis,*
> who glide-around stuffed with books with baskets-for-hand-outs
> *constant, conferunt sermones inter   sese   drapetae,* 290
> they-stand they-philosophize   among themselves renegades

---

[17] OLD 1082a s.v.

obstant,   obsistunt,   incedunt   cum suis   sententiis,
they-block   they-impede,   they-glide-around   with their wise-sayings
quos semper videas bebentes esse in thermipolio,
them always you-see drinking   in hot-drinks-shop
ubi quid subripuere – operto capitulo calidum bibunt ,
where what they-filch with-head covered hot-(drinks) they-drink
tristes atque ebrioli   incedunt –   eos ego si offendero,
somber and drunk they-glide-around them I   if bump-into
ex unoquoque eorum exciam   crepitum polentarium.
from every-one of-them I'll-knock a-noise   from-groats
("Then those robed   Greeks with their heads wrapped up,
who   go   gliding   around   stuffed   with   books   and
handout-baskets, they stand around, swap observations
between themselves, the good-for-nothings.   They block your
way, they won't let you pass, they glide around with their
pearls of wisdom.   You always see them drinking in the bars
where hot spirits are sold, where, when they've filched
something, they use it to pay for a hot drink, with their heads
wrapped up; then they glide off, all solemn – and drunk.   If I
run into them, I'll knock a bran-fed 'toot' from each one of
them.")

Plautus is on nobody's side.   He is equally hard on the Romans.   In
A Little Box the young man with a very Greek name bursts out with a
series of very Roman oaths.

Alchesimarchus.   *Enim vero   ita   me Iuppiter*
              for   indeed so-may me   Jove
itaque   me Iuno itaque Ianus ita – quid dicam nescio.   520
and-thus   me Juno and-thus Janus thus what I-will-say I-don't know
("Well then, so may Jupiter and so may Juno and so may
Janus... I forgot what I was going to say.")

There's no Zeus here. Plautus portrays different Roman neighborhoods unflatteringly. Later in *Mr. Weevil,* for no apparent reason other than Plautus' propensity for the unexpected, the company's stage manager wanders onstage (in a modern production he might be wearing street clothes and carrying a clipboard) and begins to sermonize. In Latin he is the *choragus*, a homely echo of the ΧΟΡΗΓΟΣ (khorēgos, "leader of the chorus") on the Greek stage. He methodically ticks off Roman landmarks and the characters that inhabit them, despite the fact that the play is set in Epidaurus, located in Greece proper.

> Choragus. *qui periurum convenire volt hominem ito in comitium;* 470
> whosoever perjurer meet wishes man go to assembly
> *qui mendacem et gloriosum, apud Cloacinae sacrum,*
> who liar and braggart among of-sewer temple
> *ditis damnosos maritos sub basilica quaerito...*
> rich worthless husbands beneath Basilica seek
> ("If you wish to meet a perjurer, go to the Forum's Place of Assembly; for a liar and braggart, try the temple of Venus the Purifier; for rich worthless husbands, look around the Basilica.")

The *choragus*'s neighborhoods get shadier and shadier.

> *pone aedem Castoris, ibi sunt subito quibus credas male.* 481
> behind palace of-Castor there are suddenly in-whom you-would-believe badly
> *in Tusco vico, ibi sunt homines qui ipsi sese venditant,*
> in Tuscan quarter there are people who themselves sell
> *vel qui ipsi vorsant vel qui aliis ubi vorsentur praebeant.*
> either who themselves turn-around or who for-others where are-turned-around offer
> ("Behind Castor's Temple are those whom it would be a mistake to trust too quickly. In the Tuscan Quarter are people who sell themselves – either those who roll themselves around or who let others roll them around.")

The Tuscan Quarter was along a road originally settled by Etruscans, who, by the definition cited at the beginning of this discussion, would be barbarians, too.   This "Little Etruria" features again in the blandishments – or veiled threat – of the slave Lampadio in *Mr. Weevil*.

> Lam.   *ubi tu locere in luculentam familiam,* 560
>   where you place in   bright   family
> *unde   tibi   talenta magna viginti pater*
> whence to-you talents   great twenty father
> *det   dotis;   non   enim   hic,   ubi   ex Tusco modo*
> should-give for-dowry not however here where in   Tuscan fashion
> *tute   tibi   indigne   dotem quaeras   corpore.*
> yourself for-yourself shamefully dowry you'd-seek with-body
> ("...where [I'll] place you in a squeaky-clean family, where
> your father will give you a dowry of twenty great talents; not
> like here, where you'll have to scrape up a dowry like they do
> in Little Etruria, on your back.")

Perhaps the inhabitants of Little Etruria preferred the comedies of one of Plautus' rivals.

The final incongruity involved the ultimate icon, the Roman Senate, which Plautus has somehow relocated to the Greek world.   At times the Senate is figurative, as when Epidicus muses

> Ep.   *Ite intro, ego   de   re argentaria   159*
>   go inside   I   concerning matters financial
> *iam senatum convocabo in corde consiliarium,*
> now senate I'll-convoke in heart deliberative
> ("Go inside.   As for me, I will now convoke the Senate inside
> my heart to deliberate on matters of high finance.")

In *A Little Box*, it's a place in Greece, in Sicyon.

> Lamp. *Ere, unde   is?*   776
>   heir whence   you-go
> Demphio.   *Ex senatu.*
>   from senate
> ("Boss, where are you coming from?"   "From the Senate.")

In *Epidicus* (303) the Roman Forum has also been relocated, this time to Athens.

> Apoecides.   *Quin tu is intro atque huic argentum promis?*
>   won't you go inside and for-him money get
> *ego visam ad forum.*
> I'll look to forum

("Why don't you go in and get the money for him?   Me, I'll go to the Forum and look.")

    Senati columen ("pillar of the senate") also occurs in a Greek context – that is, out of context – in *Epidicus*.

> Ep.   *iam ego me convortam in hirudinem atque eorum*
>   now I myself will-change into leech   and   of-them
> *exsugebo sanguinem,   senati   qui columen cluent.*   188
> I'll-suck   blood   of-senate   who   pillar are-known
> ("Now I'll turn into a leech and suck out the blood of those two, known as 'a pillar of the senate.'")

It also occurs in *Casina* with an equally grand epithet, but is undercut by its context, a wife's sarcastic diatribe.

> Cleostrata.   *sed eccum egreditur, senati columen, praesidium popli,*
>   but look comes-out senate's pillar guardian of-people
> *meus vicinus, meo   viro   qui liberum praehibet locum.*
> my   neighbor to-my   husband   who free offers place

("But look!   Here comes that pillar of the Senate, that guardian of the people, my neighbor, who's providing my husband with a hideaway.")

The final joke, of course, that Plautus himself was neither Greek nor Roman.   He was from Umbria, and therefore, by the definition cited at the beginning of this discussion, was a barbarian himself.

Bibliography

Adamson, Joseph, *Melville, Shame, and the Evil Eye: A Psychoanalytic Reading.* Albany. State University of New York Press, 1997.

Alexander, Philip. "How Did the Rabbis Learn Hebrew?" in Horbury, William, ed. *Hebrew Study from Ezra to Ben-Yehuda.* Edinburgh: T&T Clark, 1999.

Anonymous. *The Wanderer.* T.P. Dunning and A.J. Bliss, eds. New York. Appleton-Century-Crofts, 1969

_____. *The Seafarer.* Ida Gordon, ed. University of Exeter Press, 1996.

Barnett, Louise K. "Language, Gender, and Society in The House of Mirth." Connecticut Review 11.2 (1989).

Beaver, Harold, *American Critical Essays: Twentieth Century.* London. Oxford University Press, 1959.

Beckett, Samuel, *En Attendant Godot.* Macmillan, 1963.

Beckett, Samuel, *Waiting for Godot: Tragicomedy in 2 Acts.* Grove Press, 1982.

Bell, Millicent. "Lady into Author: Edith Wharton and the House of Scribner." American Quarterly 9 (1957).

Benstock, Shari. *No gifts from Chance: A Biography of Edith Wharton.* New York: C. Scribner's Sons, 1994.

Berlioz, Hector. *New Edition of the Complete Works.* Volume 1a. Macdonald, Hugh, ed. Bärenreiter 1987.

_____. _____. Volume 25. Holoman, D. Kern, ed. Bärenreiter 1987.

Bloom, Harold, ed. *Herman Melville's Moby-Dick.* New York. Chelsea House Publishers 1986.

Bohlke, L. Brent. "Godfrey St. Peter and Eugène Delacroix: A Portrait of the Artist in *The Professor's House*?"   Western American Literature.   May 1982.   Volume XVII, Number 1.

Bradley, S.A.J.   *Anglo-Saxon Poetry.*   Everyman, 1998.

Bristol, Marie.   "Life Among the Ungentle Genteel: Edith Wharton's The House of Mirth Revisited."   Western Humanities Review 16.4 (1962): 371-374.

Brody, Saul Nathaniel.   "Chaucer's Rhyme Royal Tales and the Secularization of the Saint."   The Chaucer Review, Vol. 20, No. 2, 1985.

Brown, Sarah and Coventry, Louise.   "Queen of Hearts: The Needs of Women with Gambling Problems."   Financial & Consumer Right Council (Victoria, Australia), 1997.

Cather, Willa.   *The Professor's House.*   Vintage Classics, 1990.

Cellini, Benvenuto.   *The Autobiography of Benvenuto Cellini.*   Symonds, John Addington, tr.   Doubleday, 1946.

_____.   _____.   *The Life of Benvenuto Cellini, A Florentine Artist Containing a variety of curious and interesting particulars, relative to painting, sculpture and architecture;   and the history of his own time. Written by himself in the Tuscan language and translated from the original, by Thomas Nugent, L.L.D., F.S.A. in two volumes. Philadelphia, Baltimore and Norfolk.*   R. and T. Desilver, 1812.

Clark, John Spencer, ed.   *The Life and Letters of John Fiske.*   (Volume II) Boston.   Houghton Mifflin   Company 1917.

Cohn, Albert.   *Shakespeare in Germany in the Sixteenth and Seventeenth Centuries: An Account of English Actors in Germany and the Netherlands and of the Plays Performed by Them During the Same Period.*   New York: Haskell House Publishers Ltd., 1971.

Collins, John J.   *Between Athens and Jerusalem: Jewish Identity in the Hellenistic Diaspora.*   Grand Rapids, Michigan: William B. Eerdmans Publishing Company, 2000.

"Comparative Vignettes of Women with Gambling Problems."   The Wager, September 1999.

Daudet, Alphonse. *Choix de Contes de Daudet.* C. Fontaine, ed. Boston, D.C. Heath, 1908.

Eisenman, Robert H., and Wise, Michael. *The Dead Sea Scrolls Uncovered: The First Complete Translation and Interpretation of 50 Key Documents Withheld for Over 35 Years.* Rockport, Massachusetts: Element, 1992.

Eliot, T.S. *The Letters of T. S. Eliot: Volume I 1898-1922..* Eliot, Valerie, ed. Harcourt Brace Jovanovich, 1988.

Eliot, T. S. *The Waste Land: A Facsimile and Transcript of the Original Drafts Including the Annotations of Ezra Pound.* Eliot, Valerie, ed. Harcourt Brace, Jovanovich, 1971.

Eliot, T. S., tr. *Anabasis: A poem by St.-John Perse, translated and with a preface by T.S. Eliot.* Harcourt BraceJovanovich, 1949.

Fabian, Ann. *Card Sharps, Dream Books, & Bucket Shops: Gambling in 19th Century America.* Cornell University Press, 1990.

Feldman, Louis H. Studies in Hellenistic Judaism. Leiden: E.J. Brill, 1996.

Fiske, John, *A History of the United States for Schools.* London. James Clarke & Co., 1894.

_____. *The Discovery of America with Some Account of Ancient America and the Spanish Conquest.* Vol. I. Boston. Houghton, Mifflin and Company, 1892.

_____. *The Unseen World.* [1876] Echo Library 2009.

Fiske, Ethel F., ed. *The Letters of John Fiske.* New York. The Macmillan Company, 1940.

"Gambling & Suicide: A Study of 44 Cases." The Wager, July 13, 1999.

Gerould, Gordon Hall. "The Second Nun's Prologue and Tale," in *Sources and Analogues of Chaucer's Canterbury Tales.* Bryan, W.F. and Dempster, Germaine, eds. Chicago: The University of Chicago Press

Giannone, Richard. *Music in Willa Cather's Fiction.* Lincoln. University of Nebraska Press, 1964.

Goldman, Irene C. "The *Perfect Jew* and *The House of Mirth*: A Study in Point of View." Modern Language Studies 23.2 (1993): 25-36.

Gordon, Lois. *The World of Samuel Beckett 1906-1946.* New Haven and London: Yale University Press, 1996.

Grennen, "Saint Cecilia's 'Chemical Wedding." The Chaucer Review, Vol. 27, No. 1, 1992.

Havel, Václav. *Living in Truth: Twenty-Two essays published on the occasion of the award of the Erasmus Prize to Václav Havel.* Vladislav, Jan, ed.   London, Faber and Faber 1989.

Hayes, Kevin J., ed. *The Critical Response to Herman Melville's Moby-Dick.* Westport, Connecticut.   Greenwood Press 1994.

Hengel, Martin, and Markschies, Christoph. *The 'Hellenization' of Judaea in the First Century after Christ.*   London: SCM Press, 1989.

Hillway, Tyrus and Mansfield, Luther S., eds. *Moby-Dick Centennial Essays.* Dallas   Southern Methodist University Press 1965.

Hirsch John C. "The Politics of Spirituality: The Second Nun and the Manciple.   The Chaucer Review, Vol. 12, No. 2, Fall 1977)

Josephus, Flavius. *The Complete Works of Josephus.*   Whiston, William, tr. Grand Rapids, Michigan: Kregel Publications, 1981.

Killoran, Helen. *Edith Wharton: Art and Allusion.*   University of Alabama Press, 1996.

Knowlson, James. *Damned to Fame: The Life of Samuel Beckett.*   New York: Simon & Schuster 1996.

Krauss, Samuel. *Griechische und Lateinische Lehnwörter im Talmud, Midrasch und Targum.*   Hildesheim: Georg   Olms Verlagsbuchhandlung, 1964.

Larson, Ken.   "Shakespeare between Aufklärung and Sturm und Drang." aurora.wells.edu/klarson

Lenin, Vladimir Ilych. *Collected Works.*   Moscow: Foreign Languages Publishing House 1963.

Levine, Lee I. *Judaism and Hellenism in Antiquity: Conflict or Confluence?* Seattle & London: University of Washington Press, 1998.

Lewis, R.W.B. *Edith Wharton: A Biography.*   Harper and Row, 1975.

Lin, Yutang. *The Secret Name.*   New York: Farrar, Straus and Cudahy 1958.

Longsworth, Robert M.   "Privileged Knowledge: St. Cecilia and the Alchemist in the *Canterbury Tales.* The Chaucer Review, Vol. 27, No. 1, 1992.

Lubbock, Percy. *Portrait of Edith Wharton.* Appleton-Century, 1947.

March, John. *A Reader's Companion to the Fiction of Willa Cather.* Westport, Connecticut. Greenwood Press, 1993.

Markels, Julian, *Melville and the Politics of Identity: From King Lear to Moby-Dick.* Urbana. University of Illinois Press 1993.

McCarthy, Paul, *"The Twisted Mind:" Madness in Herman Melville's Fiction.* Iowa City. University of Iowa Press, 1990.

McDowell, Margaret B. *Edith Wharton.* Twayne Publishers, 1991.

Melville, Herman, *Billy Budd, Sailor and Other Stories.* Beaver, Harold, ed. Harmondsworth, Middlesex, England 1973

_____. *Moby-Dick or, The Whale.* Feidelson, Charles Jr., ed. Indianapolis. Bobbs-Merrill 1964.

_____. *Moby-Dick or, The Whale.* Mansfield, Luther S. and Vincent, Howard P., eds. New York. Hendricks House, 1952.

_____. *Moby Dick.* Tanner, Tony, ed. Oxford. Oxford University Press 1988.

Nevill, Ralph. *Light come, Light Go: Gambling—Gamesters—Wagers— the Turf.* MacMillan, 1909.

Newman, William R. , *The* Summa Perfectionis *of Pseudo-Geber: A Critical Edition, Translation and Study.* Brill, 1991.

Nixon, Paul. *Plautus II.* The Loeb Classical Library. New York: G.P. Putnam's Sons, 1917.

Ogilvie, R. M. *Roman Literature and Society.* New York: Penguin, 1980.

Palisca, Claude V. *Baroque Music.* Prentice-Hall, 1968.

Palmer, L. R. *The Latin Language.* Norman: University of Oklahoma Press, 1988.

Paper, Herbert H., ed. *Jewish Languages: Theme and Variations.* Cambridge, Massachusetts: Association for Jewish Studies, 1978.

Patai, Raphael, *The Jewish Alchemists: A History and Source Book.* Princeton University Press, 1994.

Peterson, Elmer, *Tristan Tzara: Dada and Surrational Theorist.* Rutgers University Press, 1971.

Priesner, Claus and Figala, Karin, eds., Alchemie: Lexikon einer hermetischen Wissenschaft. C. H. Beck, 1998.

Robillard, Douglas. *Melville and the Visual Arts: Ionian Form, Venetian Tint*. The Kent State University Press, 1992.

Ruška, Julius, "Studien zu Muhammad Ibn Umail al-Tamimi's Kitāb al-Ma' al-Waraqi wa'l-Ard an-Najmiyah." Isis, p.310

Schlegel, August Wilhelm. *Kritische Schriften, Ausgewählt, Eingeleitet und Erläutert von Emil Staiger*. Zürich und Stuttgart. Artemis Verlag, 1962.

_____. *Kritische Schriften und Briefe VII*. Edgar Lohner, ed. Stuttgart. Verlag W. Kohlhammer, 1974.

_____. *Vorlesungen über Äesthetik I. Mit Kommentar und Nachwort*. Ernst Behler, ed. Paderborn. Ferdinand Schönigh, 1989.

Saroyan, William. *The Human Comedy*. New York: Dell, 1971.

Sealts, Merton M., Jr. *Melville's Reading*. University of South Carolina Press, 1988.

Shakespeare, William. *W. Shakespeares dramatische Werke / uebersetzt von Aug. Wilh. von Schlegel und Ludw. Tieck: im Auftrag der Deutschen Shakespeare-Gesellschaft herausgegeben und mit Einleitungen versehen von Wilhelm Oechelhäuser*. Stuttgart; Leipzig, Deutsche Verlags-Anstalt [1905].

Skupin, Michael. "Colloquial Carthaginian." Epigraphic Society Occasional Papers,19:188-201

_____. "Shakespeare in the EFL Classroom." Proceedings of *Renderings: Shakespeare across Continents*. University of Nottingham, Ningbo, China (forthcoming).

Skupin, Michael and Wu, Theresa L. "Latin, Finally!" Proceedings of 2007 Conference on English Learning and Teaching: Linking Theory with Practice." Crane, 2007.

Soukup, Rudolf Werner and Mayer, Helmut, *Alchemistisches Gold: Paracelsistische Pharmaka*. Böhlau, 1997.

Sperber, Daniel. *A Dictionary of Greek and Latin Legal Terms in Rabbinic Literature*. Bar-Ilan Press, 1984.

Todd, Jeff, "Ahab and the Glamour of Evil: A Burkean Reading of Ritual in Moby Dick." Papers on Language & Literature Volume 33, Number 1, Winter 1997.

Tzara, Tristan. *Œvres Complètes.* Vols. 1 & 2. Béhar, Henri, ed. Flammarion, 1975.

Vermorcken, Elizabeth Moorhead. Pittsburgh Portraits. Pittsburgh: Boxwood Press, 1955,

Wacholder, Ben Zion and Abegg, Martin G., eds. *A Preliminary Edition of the Unpublished Dead Sea Scrolls: The Hebrew and Aramaic Texts from Cave Four, Fascicle One.* Washington, D.C.: Biblical Archaeology Society, 1991.

Weinreich, Uriel. *Modern English-Yiddish Yiddish-English Dictionary.* Schocken Books, 1977.

Wharton, Edith. *A Backward Glance.* Century, 1987.

Wharton, Edith. *The House of Mirth.* Lewis, R.W.B., ed. Houghton-Mifflin, 1963.

Wigram, George V. *The Englishman's Hebrew and Chaldee Concordance of the Old Testament.* Grand Rapids, Michigan. Baker Book House, 1980.

Wilson, James Grant, and Fiske, John, eds. *Appleton's Cyclopædia of American Biography.* Volume II. New York. D. Appleton and Company 1894.

Wolf, Cynthia Griffin. *A Feast of Words: The Triumph of Edith Wharton.* Oxford University Press, 1977.

Women Gamblers. Arizona Council on Compulsive Gambling, 1999. azccg@azccg.org.

Yongue, Patricia Lee, "Search and Research: Willa Cather in Quest of History." Southwestern American Literature 5 (1975). 27-39.

語言文學類　AG0120

Loose Ends in Western Literature

作　　者 / Michael Skupin
發 行 人 / 宋政坤
執行編輯 / 詹靚秋
圖文排版 / 鄭維心
封面設計 / 陳佩蓉
數位轉譯 / 徐真玉　沈裕閔
圖書銷售 / 林怡君
法律顧問 / 毛國樑　律師
出版印製 / 秀威資訊科技股份有限公司
　　　　　 臺北市內湖區瑞光路 583 巷 25 號 1 樓
　　　　　 電話：02-2657-9211　　　　傳真：02-2657-9106
　　　　　 E-mail：service@showwe.com.tw
經 銷 商 / 紅螞蟻圖書有限公司
　　　　　 臺北市內湖區舊宗路二段 121 巷 28、32 號 4 樓
　　　　　 電話：02-2795-3656　　　　傳真：02-2795-4100
　　　　　 http://www.e-redant.com

2009 年 12 月 BOD 一版
定價：230 元

讀　者　回　函　卡

感謝您購買本書，為提升服務品質，煩請填寫以下問卷，收到您的寶貴意見後，我們會仔細收藏記錄並回贈紀念品，謝謝！

1.您購買的書名：＿＿＿＿＿＿＿＿＿＿＿＿＿＿＿＿＿＿

2.您從何得知本書的消息？

　　□網路書店　　□部落格　　□資料庫搜尋　　□書訊　　□電子報　　□書店

　　□平面媒體　　□ 朋友推薦　　□網站推薦　□其他＿＿＿＿＿＿

3.您對本書的評價：(請填代號　1.非常滿意 2.滿意 3.尚可 4.再改進)

　　封面設計＿＿＿　版面編排＿＿＿　內容＿＿＿　文/譯筆＿＿＿　價格＿＿＿

4.讀完書後您覺得：

　　□很有收獲　　□有收獲　　□收獲不多　　□沒收獲

5.您會推薦本書給朋友嗎？

　　□會　　□不會，為什麼？＿＿＿＿＿＿＿＿＿＿＿＿＿＿＿＿＿＿

6.其他寶貴的意見：＿＿＿＿＿＿＿＿＿＿＿＿＿＿＿＿＿＿＿＿＿

＿＿＿＿＿＿＿＿＿＿＿＿＿＿＿＿＿＿＿＿＿＿＿＿＿＿＿＿＿＿＿＿＿

＿＿＿＿＿＿＿＿＿＿＿＿＿＿＿＿＿＿＿＿＿＿＿＿＿＿＿＿＿＿＿＿＿

＿＿＿＿＿＿＿＿＿＿＿＿＿＿＿＿＿＿＿＿＿＿＿＿＿＿＿＿＿＿＿＿＿

讀者基本資料

姓名：＿＿＿＿＿＿＿＿＿＿　年齡：＿＿＿＿　性別：□女 □男

聯絡電話：＿＿＿＿＿＿＿＿＿　E-mail：＿＿＿＿＿＿＿＿＿＿＿

地址：＿＿＿＿＿＿＿＿＿＿＿＿＿＿＿＿＿＿＿＿＿＿＿＿＿＿＿

學歷：□高中(含)以下　　□高中　　□專科學校　　□大學

　　　□研究所(含)以上 □其他＿＿＿＿＿＿＿＿

職業：□製造業 □金融業 □資訊業 □軍警 □傳播業 □自由業

　　　□服務業 □公務員 □教職　　□學生 □其他＿＿＿＿＿＿

To：114

台北市內湖區瑞光路 583 巷 25 號 1 樓

秀威資訊科技股份有限公司　　　收

寄件人姓名：

寄件人地址：□□□

(請沿線對摺寄回,謝謝!)

秀威與 BOD

BOD（Books On Demand）是數位出版的大趨勢，秀威資訊率先運用 POD 數位印刷設備來生產書籍，並提供作者全程數位出版服務，致使書籍產銷零庫存，知識傳承不絕版，目前已開闢以下書系：

一、BOD 學術著作—專業論述的閱讀延伸
二、BOD 個人著作—分享生命的心路歷程
三、BOD 旅遊著作—個人深度旅遊文學創作
四、BOD 大陸學者—大陸專業學者學術出版
五、POD 獨家經銷—數位產製的代發行書籍

BOD 秀威網路書店：www.showwe.com.tw
政府出版品網路書店：www.govbooks.com.tw

永不絕版的故事・自己寫・永不休止的音符・自己唱